Erotica Taboo Sex Stories

Hot Explicit Erotic Stories Including First Time, Family, Blowjobs, Bisexual, Gangbangs, Forbidden, Rough, and Many More

Angelo Wilson

rendering of legal, financial, medical or professional advice. The content within this book has been derived from various sources. Please consult a licensed professional before attempting any techniques outlined in this book.

By reading this document, the reader agrees that under no circumstances is the author responsible for any losses, direct or indirect, that are incurred as a result of the use of the information contained within this document, including, but not limited to, errors, omissions, or inaccuracies.

Table of Contents

Table of Contents 3

In the Office 4

My Lucky Day 32

A Blue Summer Dress 51

First Lesbian Sex 65

An Existential Crisis 88

His Cock Twitching in the Air 103

The Most Wonderful Weekend 138

Sex with Laila 155

My First Threesome 169

The MILF Nurse and The Hot Biker 181

A Straightforward MFM Threesom 204

The BBW 217

A BDSM Munch 234

In the Office

Millicent Jamison scanned the job offers page on her laptop. This has been a regular habit since she was fired from the Peerless Upholstery Company. She loved her job as general manager of the office, taking phone enquiries, booking deadlines and a hundred other tasks that made her days interesting and varied. Now that her husband, Stephen, has been on short notice, she was desperate to find a new position. So far, she has not been able to find anything to suit her experience. At 49, Millicent did not want to completely change her career path.

Come on, bingo! That must be it, she thought that since her eyes were focused on the vacancy, which looked like it was made for her:

"A small family business with old-fashioned values is looking for a general manager of the office who will take care of bookings, appointments, welcome customers and a lot of other duties. Salaries to be negotiated, according to experience. Please submit your application together with your CV and two references to Paradise Tanners under heading number XX1".

Feeling excited and more positive than for centuries, Millicent wrote a cover letter and attached its impressive CV. The references were joined by Mr Brockleban, CEO of Peerless Upholstery, and Mrs Wandless, President of the local Mother's Association branch.

Ten days later a letter came from Paradise Tanners informing Millicent that she had been selected for the post and invited her to an interview. My luck is changing, Millicent told herself.

On the day of the interview she wore an elegant suit in a style that she thought would match the "old-fashioned values" advertised by Paradise Tanners. Millicent was a little surprised when she arrived at the address given in the job interview letter. It was quite a large, Victorian semi-detached house, nothing seemed to indicate that it was a business address. With its exuberant net curtains and a potted plant in the bay window, it was very similar to all other houses on the street. How strange. Millicent was expecting a small factory or unit in a business park, like her old company.

Millicent rang the doorbell and after a few moments you answered her about 40 years later. "Oh, you must be Mrs. Jamison. Welcome to Paradise Tanners. I'm Mrs. Paradise, this way, please." Millicent was brought into the cozy front room and invited to sit on the couch.

"I've read your resume, Mrs Jamison, and I must say I'm impressed. I also spoke on the phone with Mr. Brocklebank, and he spoke most about you. You seem to have all the qualities we're looking for. Before we move on, maybe I should ask you what you know about our business, Paradise Tanners."

Millicent was blushing. She really didn't know anything about the company. She assumed it had to be about leather goods. Mrs. Paradise smiled at the inconvenience of Millicent. "I think I should explain. When we announced this position, we were rather discreet and did not reveal the true nature of what we were doing." Millicent's face fell, wondering what she could afford.

"Oh, don't worry Mrs. Jamison, it's not illegal. We don't

grow weeds or anything. But this is something we have to be careful about. The thing is, Paradise Tanners make movies with spanking. We spank ladies' asses and film them. We sell them as DVDs or publish them on the Internet. It's perfectly legal, but of course we have to be very discreet."

"Oh, I see," said Millicent Jamison, surprised. "What would I have to do, Mrs. Paradise."

"Well, just what we put in the ad; answering phones, making bookings, keeping files and generally making sure the office is running smoothly. You wouldn't have to get involved in spanking." "You wouldn't have to get involved in spanking. And then I add, "unless you're obviously interested in this website."

God, that's not what Millicent expected when she applied for this job. But what a pity, she justified it. She'd be happy to fill in by updating her calendar, answering her phone and making coffee. If the ladies got spanked in another room, what did it matter?

"Well, Mrs. Jamison, now you know a little more about us, would you still want this job?"

"Yes, ma'am, Mrs. Raj. When do you want me to start?"

"Will Monday suit you? We're expecting quite a busy week."

Millicent was a little vague when her husband asked about her new job. "Oh, general office work, just like my previous job," she answered his question.

On Monday, with a mixture of nervousness and excitement, Millicent arrived at Paradise Tanners ten minutes earlier. She was received by Mrs. Paradise. "Call me Sylvia," she said. "We are like family here at Paradise Tanners. Come with me and I'll show you around."

Sylvia took Millicent to the living room where she was interrogated. "This is the room we use for home scenes, such as the daughter coming home at midnight, two hours after curfew. She has to go through Daddy's knee. You can imagine the scene, I'm sure of it."

Millicent, wanting to show interest in her new job, she said: "Oh yes, Sylvia, I remember one evening I came home a little late and went over Daddy's knee." Sylvia, she looked at her new employee with new interest.

"Oh, you have some experience with being flogged, so?"

Millicent started regretting her impulsive attention. "Just a few times," she assured her new boss.

Sylvia moved to another room. "This is the school room." The room had a whiteboard, a teacher's desk, a few student benches, a wooden stool with a headgear and other school accessories, including a range of sticks. The third room was quite a conventional bedroom. Finally, Sylvia showed Millicent the study where she was to live and the waiting room, which was rather similar to the one in the doctor's study.

"This is where you should ask the ladies who come in for spanking to wait until we're ready for them. I'll tell you a little trade secret here, Millicent. We have a rule of thumb for the ladies to always wait a little, even if we're ready for their visit. "Waiting increases their anxiety and builds tension."

When the tour was over, Sylvia left Millicent in her office. "Your first task will be to welcome Joanne Thimble." Sylvia was looking at her watch. "She should be here in half an hour. She's a newcomer who answered one of our announcements. She's gonna have a spanking audition that I'm gonna run. If everything goes well, maybe she'll come back for a more intensive session. Make her coffee and show her in the waiting room. You can direct her to the waiting room when I'm ready. I'll call you on the intercom." The intercom was a model similar to the one Millicent used in her previous job.

Mrs. Thimble arrived fifteen minutes before her meeting. Millicent was surprised at what she looked like, just like a hundred other middle-class housewives. "Oh, I'm sorry, I know I'm quite early, but I wasn't sure about the address. I hope I'm not bothering you."

Millicent made good use of her people, assuring Mrs Thimble that everything was all right and took her to the waiting room.

"Do you want a cup of tea or coffee?"

"Oh, coffee would be lovely. Just a drop of milk and no sugar."

When Millicent brought the coffee a few minutes later, Mrs. Thimble was nervously playing with her purse. "Er, you'll, umm," she got stammed up. "Er, will you, umm, spank?"

"Me"? Oh, God, no. No, I think it'll be Mrs. Paradise. She'll call in a minute."

Just then, Millicent heard a noise at the back door. She went to the investigation, leaving Mrs. Thimble alone with her coffee. A middle-aged man, carrying a big bag, just walked into the building. "Hello, you must be the new office manager. I'm Cecil Paradise."

"Nice to meet you, Mr. Paradise. I'm Millicent Jamison. Mrs. Thimble is here for questioning."

"Oh, good. My better half does the honors. I'm an operator this morning. I'd better go and set up the equipment, or I'll get smacked." Cecil Paradise, grabbing his own joke, fell into the living room with his equipment.

Millicent returned to the waiting room. "Is the coffee all right, Mrs. Thimble?"

"Yes, fine, thank you. Please call me Joanne."

"So, Joanne, I'm sure they'll be ready for you soon. It'll be Mrs Paradise to spank you while Mr Paradise films it."

"Oh, I see." Joanne blushed. "This is my first time. I'm a little nervous."

I never would have guessed, Millicent thought. "I'm sure you'll be fine, Joanne."

"I really hope so. I was looking forward to a new experience, but now I'm here to do it. well, I have to admit I'm a little scared.

Millicent was about to offer further reassurance when a woman's voice came over the intercom. "please show joanne thimble to the rec room."

After guiding Joanne through the lounge to meet Mrs. Paradise in the lounge, Millicent returned to her office to inspect the equipment. There were all the usual office paraphernalia found in any small office: computers, staplers, paper clips, a paper cup with pens and pencils, a telephone, etc. Then their attention turned to a television screen. It was divided into quarters to transmit the video footage from a number of security cameras. One showed the front door, another the back door, and the other two quarters were just gray panels. Obviously, they were not in use.

As Millicent moved her office chair, a sudden movement on the screen caught her eye. A third quarter of the screen had suddenly become active. A camera panned around in the lounge, shifting the focus from a blur to a sharper image. Millicent noticed that Mr. Paradise had his camera on, and it was set to transmit the view to the monitor screen. Gradually, the view calmed down and showed Mrs. Paradise and Joanne sitting at the table.

Millicent knew she should turn away. She felt guilty as she watched the scene in the lounge. Something forced her to keep looking. There was no sound, just the black-and-white picture. The scene changed when the two women stood up. Millicent's heart raced when she saw Madame Paradise pulling up Joanne's dress. Mr. Paradise adjusted the camera lens to zoom in on Joanne's lace-clad black panties.

Mrs. Paradise's hand raised and lowered itself, striking Joanne's lace-covered black buttocks, a tattoo. Millicent swallowed hard and felt Mrs Paradise's humiliation out of pity for Mrs Foxglove. Then Mrs. Paradise pulled Joanne's panties down and revealed the pale flesh that had just begun to take on a pinkish red colour. Millicent blushed when she thought about how grateful she was that it was Joanne who got spanked and not her. What was the German word that summed up the feeling of enjoying someone's discomfort rather than being compassionate? Oh, yes, that's it; "Schadenfreude."

Joanne began to fidget and squirm. Obviously, Mrs. Paradise made an impression on the inexperienced woman Foxglove. Then, oh God! Millicent instinctively put a hand to her mouth in shock. Mrs. Thimble had chosen a leather device shaped like a ping-pong paddle and began to slap Mrs. Thimble on her bare bottom. Mr. Paradise had zoomed Mrs. Thimble's bottom very close. Her legs were spread and revealed the maroon fluff that adorned her matronly slit.

Millicent swallowed hard. She was shocked, but undeniably tickled by her voyeuristic gaze. She herself was surprised at how much she enjoyed Joanne's discomfort in the hands of the formidable woman Paradise.

Schadenfreude!

At last the ordeal was over. Frau Fingerhut rubbed her sore bottom before pulling up her panties and straightening her frock. Guiltily, Millicent turned off the monitor and, while trying to control her breathing, waited for Joanne to come out of the lounge. As she came out, she gave Millicent a faint smile.

"Was everything all right, Mrs Thimble?"

"Uh, very invigorating, my dear."

After Mrs Thimble left, Mrs Paradise came into the office.

"Millicent, I would like you to add Joanne Thimble to

our database. Complete today's entry and find an opening for next week. Our Mrs. Thimble is a natural talent for spanking videos, she has a perfect backside that was made to be spanked. Next time her Mr. Paradise will introduce her favorite belt.

"Why, certainly, Mrs Paradise. No problem, mrs. Paradise. I'm completely familiar with Microsoft Office. I'm sure your database will present no problems."

"Good, and when you've done that, pull up the file on Kandy Kreme. (That's with two K's, by the way). She's going to be on camera this afternoon for a scene Kandy is a total bitch, but very much in demand by our clients. She is 29 years old, but can pass for a college student in a short skirt and white blouse".

Curiously, Millicent brought up the database entries and searched Kandy Kreme. From the number of entries, it was immediately clear that Ms. Kreme was a very productive artist. There were several images included that showed her in some of her roles. Millicent added Joanne Jamison to the database and closed the system. She noted that she should ask Mr. or Mrs.

Paradise for a picture for Joanne's database entry.

Kandy arrived exactly on time. She was wearing a long coat, which she left in the waiting room. She was wearing a tiny tartan skirt that revealed her white cotton panties every time she moved.

"You must be new," she watched as she checked Millicent up and down.

"Yes, hello, I'm Millicent, delighted to meet you. I'm the new office manager."

"Oh, yes," Kandy said. "I was wondering if you were here to get your ass kicked." Then she demonstratively removed a pack of gum from her mouth that she had been chewing all along since she arrived.

"Sorry about the gum, but it's part of the script for my scene."

"Screenplay?" Millicent looked confused.

"Yeah. Not much of a script, really. The idea is that Mr Paradise catches me sticking it under my desk and decides to beat my naked butt with a rod.

"sounds like a pretty harsh punishment for something as trivial as sticking gum under your desk."

"Yeah, any excuse to get my drawers down. Besides, I have a reputation to uphold for my fans. I am the ultimate bad girl. I have to be naughty and get spanked to keep my fan base.

"Doesn't it hurt to get your naked butt spanked?"

"I'd say it does, but there's pride in a job well done. It fills me with satisfaction that I can do it without screaming. A lot of the girls scream and cry at the first spanking, but not Kandy Kreme. I think Mr. Paradise is frustrated that he can't get me to scream for mercy. Of course I squirm a little. The fans like it when I wiggle my butt after each stroke. And, oh, yeah, the money's good too. Better than working."

Then a stern voice came over the intercom. "Miss Kreme, get over here right away."

"It's happening again, and the marks of my last beating have not quite disappeared."

As soon as Kandy Kreme went to Mr Paradise, Millicent turned on the monitor, hoping the scene would play out. She thought she was very much looking forward to seeing Kandy's performance.

The camera zoomed in on Kandy's right hand while she pressed a pack of gum into the desk cover. Then she panned to an angry looking Mr. Paradise, who seemed to be protesting with a rebellious Kandy Kreme with standing Armakimbo. Millicent wished she could hear what was being said.

Mr. Paradise grabbed Kandy and in a fake outburst of

rage, tore her across his knee. Her short skirt was pulled up, revealing the tight-fitting white panties that were tucked over her round bottom. Millicent's heart raced as Mr. Paradise began to slap Kandy on the ass, first on one cheek, then the other. It was obvious the man was deadly serious. He seemed determined to force his favorite victim to surrender and beg for mercy.

Mr. Paradise grabbed the waistband of the cotton panties and peeled them down to his thighs, depriving Kandy of any protection. The slaps continued raining in a moderate rhythm. Even with the limitations of the black and white monitor, Millicent could see that the young woman's buttocks were turning color.

Then Mr. Paradise allowed Kandy to stand up. He pointed to something that was not on the screen, and Kandy moved out of the shot, returned a few moments later, carrying a stick, and handed it to Mr. Paradise.

Almost ashamed of the voyeuristic pleasure she was getting from watching, Millicent's eyes were riveted to the screen. She watched as Kandy bent down as Mr. Paradise pushed the cane through the air with a few practice strokes. Then, with careful aiming, the first blow landed on Kandy's expelled floor. The impact made the young woman's pale flesh tremble, and a clear line appeared clean above her buttocks.

Mr. Paradise paused and let the full effect work before lifting the stick for a second blow. Millicent pressed his thighs together in anticipation of the next stroke landing. She wondered why this dirty scene had such an effect on her. She was shocked at the sexual excitement Candy's suffering caused her.

As several more strokes landed with infallible accuracy, a series of clean parallel lines marked Candy's beautiful bottom. Millicent rubbed the area between her thighs, and when the camera zoomed in and the delicious butt filled the screen, she had an incredible orgasm.

The slapping finally came to an end and Kandy had to go to the "corner of shame" with her skirt up to show her tube-striped butt.

Millicent was very thoughtful as she started to walk home.

"How did the new job go today, Millie?" Millicent's husband, Stephen, looked over his glasses and put down the Racing Gazette for a moment.

"Oh, fine, thanks, Steve. I'm just getting into the swing of things." Stephen grunted without obligation. He was back studying the odds of the 3.30 Doncaster race.

"Were you ever tempted to spank me, Steve?"

"Why did you do that?"

"Oh, nothing dear. I just wondered."

For the rest of the week, women of all ages, shapes and sizes came to Paradise Tanner to get spanked. One rather buxom lady in her late 40s looked familiar, although her name - Betty Boobs - didn't mean anything. Millicent couldn't quite place her. When she was in the studio and Millicent was watching on the monitor, the buxom woman proudly and confidently showed her huge tits and big ass. The penny dropped - it was the woman who ran the underwear stand in the market hall. In addition to conventional underwear, she kept a number of exotic underpants, some of which she had just disposed of.

Mr. Paradise lost no time when he started working on his tits and bottom with a small leather paddle. Betty Boobs was obviously no stranger to being treated in this way by men. In fact, she seemed to enjoy the treatment that Mr Paradise gave her.

Mr. Paradise must be having the best time of his life, Millicent thought, especially when Betty fell to her knees to suck Mr. Paradise's penis. Meanwhile, Mrs. Paradise allowed the camera to continue filming. This was to be a special production.

Millicent was more and more fascinated by the activities at Paradise Tanner. To say that she was tempted to try it herself was perhaps overstating the case. That is, until she had updated the accounts on the spreadsheet. She noticed that Kandy Kreme had earned more in an hour than she would earn for a whole working day. Why not give it a try, just once? It couldn't hurt, could it?

Millicent plucked up the courage to approach Mrs. Paradise. "Sylvia, I was wondering if I could have an audition to get spanked."

Sylvia curiously glanced at her office manager. "Well, I don't see why not. Your predecessor has succumbed to temptation; we can try if you'd like. Just a word of warning: Mr Paradise and I do not treat our staff lightly. They get exactly the same treatment as the other ladies, a good thrashing on the bare bottom. Do you think you can handle that, Millicent?"

"I think so, Sylvia.

"Very well, Millicent, perhaps you should make an appointment.

Millicent could feel her heartbeat when she booked an appointment in an empty seat.

She had noticed that most of the ladies in her age group wore stockings with suspenders during spanking sessions. Millicent couldn't remember the last time she had worn them, but she found them in her underwear drawer. When the day arrived, Millicent felt a mixture of excitement and nervousness.

The morning dragged on as Millicent filled her time with trivial tasks and waited for her 2 pm appointment. It's like waiting for a dental checkup, only worse, she told herself. Eventually, the appointed time came.

"Mrs. Jamison, please come into the parlor." Millicent, swallowed hard and entered the lounge. Mrs. Paradise was behind the camera, which was mounted on a tripod. Mr Paradise rose from the sofa on which he had sat and greeted his employee in her new role as Spankee.

"Millicent, are you still glad to be able to continue? If

you've changed your mind, that's perfectly all right."

"no, mr. Paradise, i haven't changed my mind. I'm happy to go on."

"very well. Did you sign the release form?" It was a rule that all ladies had to agree in writing to corporal punishment before each session. Millicent confirmed that her signed consent form was on file. She confirmed that she agreed to receive corporal punishment on her bare bottom by hand, strap and stick,

"In this case, I think we'll start with a standard above the knee warm-up. Please go above my knee, Millicent." Ms. Paradise began recording the session when Millicent was above her employer's knee.

"Ouch!" The first slap over her dress came as a shock. It hurt more than she expected. I must pull myself together, she said to herself. The beating hasn't really started yet. Millicent managed to take the next few slaps without shame, although a fire began to smoulder in her best panties made of creamy lace.

"Time to remove some of your protection." Mr. Paradise pulled Millicent's dress up to her waist, revealing her stocking-clad legs and pretty panties. He grunted his approval of the enticing target. The warm-up continued as slaps continued to rain down on the panty-covered buttocks. Mr. Paradise smiled to himself as the woman above his lap began to writhe in discomfort. After a few minutes, he decided it was time to strip Millicent of her last layer of protection.

Millicent was relieved after the temporary pause for breath when her tormentor interrupted the beating as he cautiously began to loosen her panties in his butt. He pulled her across her hips to a position midway between her buttocks and knees. He examined Millicent's buttocks carefully and noticed that the previously pale, alabaster-colored flesh took on a pretty pink color. His experience told him that the pink would soon turn into bruises. Ms. Jamison's inexperience made her particularly vulnerable. At this stage of a beating, Kandy Kreme or Betty Boobs would have barely visible marks. Millicent couldn't remember the last time anyone but her husband pulled her underwear down. Basically, she couldn't remember the last time her husband pulled her underwear down.

The beating continued with the sound of flesh on flesh as the beater's hand met the naked cheeks of the naked behind. Mrs. Jamison did her best to keep her thighs closed and tried to avoid exposing her furry female charms. She had noticed how the ladies almost always exposed themselves when they were spanked. So Millicent held her legs tightly together.

Unfortunately, as Millicent was to find out, a serious spanking comes at a time when it's no longer a matter of maintaining one's dignity. The struggle to avoid the burning pain is exhausting. When she felt the heat, she began to wriggle and squirm, trying in vain to escape the agony. Mrs. Paradise was able to take many revealing pictures between Millicent's thighs. She desperately tried to protect her bottom with her hands, but Mr. Paradise was too experienced a wrench for that. He controlled her arms slightly with one hand while he continued the blows with the other.

"Okay, that's enough. You can stand up now, Ms.

Jamison, but hold your dress up. We all want to see your bottom." Millicent came to her feet wobbly and carefully felt her bottom, convinced that, judging by the terrible burning, it must be badly damaged. At Mr. Paradise's request, she stood in the corner of the room facing the wall while holding up her dress in favor of the camera.

"Don't worry, there's no harm done, although your pretty ass will look pretty bruised tomorrow and may be a little tender. I think we should end our session here for now. If you want to experience the kiss of a leather strap or the sting of a stick, please sign up for another session. I am sure Mrs Paradise or myself would be happy to help you.

"did you have a good day at work, millie ?" Stephen Jamison looked up from the Racing Gazette.

"Oh, not bad love, not bad at all. You know how it is, all jobs have their ups and downs. Sometimes it's great, and some days it can be a real pain in the ass."

Stephen giggled. "To true love. You got that right." He turned back to his paper. "Shit! Charlie Boy at Newmarket let me down. "If I'd been romping around the square, I'd have been fifty pounds overweight. He's a real pain in the ass!"

My Lucky Day

I stood there feeling so nervous I felt like I could break down at any moment. The anxiety was `hitting me like a freight train as I clenched my hand tightly around Brandon's arm. I think he could tell by the way I was digging my nails into him that I was having another one of these moments. He loosened my grip on his arm and took my hand in his. "Do we need to step out a moment, Rhia?" he asked me.

I bit my lip, because I didn't want to have to say yes. "Yes," I said to him. He nodded reassuringly as we quietly slipped out of the hotel lobby. The competition was about to begin soon and as usual, my nerves were getting the best of me. I had already competed and won in the regional championships through hard work and Brandon's support. I hate that I am having to rely on it once again. Well, hate is a strong word, because I definitely don't hate what we do.

Brandon was already working his way through college, but he took the time off of classes for the day to make sure everything ran smoothly for me in this competition. It was to be televised and everything! Local and internationally famous chefs were showing up as judges and I was to be competing against other champion amateur chefs for the big prize, a fully paid college tuition to culinary school paid for by the famous Chef Roland, a television celebrity who lived right here in Michigan. There had even been rumors the winner would be slated a job at one of his restaurants should they succeed through college. I knew I was good enough to win, and I knew I wanted it more than anyone else. I've been practicing and honing my skills in the kitchen for years just for this moment. The last thing I could afford was letting my nerves get to me. Brandon knew the most effective way to help me deal with the anxiety though, and that was a good, quick fuck.

"Here we are," he said as he nodded to restroom sign for the Men's bathroom.

I gagged a little. "Are you crazy? It's a public bathroom!" I whispered loudly at him.

He chuckled and looked around. "No one is on this hall watching, it will be quick, now come on, babe," he said to me. I did like it when he called me babe, and I guess he is right, no one is watching.

I looked around one last time with him and nodded. "Okay, but let's make this quick," I told him.

He gave me a sly wink as he pulled me by the hand into the bathroom. We closed the door behind us and I am giggling at the idea of sneaky public sex. I could still feel the heavy build-up of anxiety welled up inside of me but it immediately begins to dissipate as he wrapped his hands around my waist and kissed me. I wasted no time in guiding his hands up my flat stomach and over my breasts. I breathed heavily as we move towards one of the stalls, away from the door. I looked at myself in the mirror smiling as I wrapped my arms around Brandon and he kissed on my neck and nipped at my skin. I felt his hands caress my breasts through my bra and my nipples became harder at the sensation. He pulled down my bra under my shirt and flicked my nipples just so he could get me to squirm in his arms. He was good at making me do that.

Knowing we had to move quickly, I decided to undo his pants and pull out his fully erect cock. He watched me pull away as I moved down on him and took his throbbing hard-on in my mouth. I sucked on him for several seconds to get a good lubrication on his shaft before standing and smirking at him. He smirked back as he turned me around. I leaned against the wall as he pulled my pants down and exposed my ass for him to see. I bent over more to show him my wet pussy as he pushed himself deep inside my walls. I immediately let out a moan of pleasure as he pushed in and out slowly. "Faster," I commanded him. It felt amazing, but we didn't have that much time to waste.

Like the good man he is, Brandon obliged as he

proceeded to thrust harder into me. Our exposed bodies clapped against each other as I made an effort to push back against his cock. I licked my fingers and guided them down between my legs to find my clitoris. It was hard and pulsating already from the pleasure as I circled my wet fingers around it. I wanted to cum and cum hard for Brandon. We just had to mind our time. He slapped my ass and got really into it as I could hear him breathing heavily as he mumbled my name. I liked that he did that. That was usually enough to help get me off.

It was at that moment the door opened and we both turned and froze. My heart sank as we were right there in the middle of the bathroom fucking for anyone who walked in to see. My heart sank, even more, when I recognized the man who walked in. Chef Roland, the Michigan born celebrity chef who was judging today's competition. He looked at the two of us as we stood there, frozen. Brandon was still inside of me as I could feel his body clenched in fear. Chef Roland raised a brow looking at me. "You're one of the competitors in today's competition, are you not?" he said as he looked square at me with a knowing grin on his face.

"Sir, this isn't what it looks like!" I said to him. I'm not sure why, because it was exactly what it looked like.

"Are you sure about that?" he said as he walked closer

to us. Brandon pulled out and pulled his pants up nervously as I did the same. Chef Roland shook his head. "I think it's very clear what is going on here. You two a bunch of exhibitionists?"

Brandon and I looked at each other, petrified. "Something like that, sir," I heard Brandon say as I am staring at the admittingly very handsome celebrity looking at us.

"Please, Chef Roland," I said through a stuttering of tears. "I'll do anything to stay in the competition. My boyfriend, he was just helping me calm my nerves. I really wanted to do well but I have anxiety and-" He raised his hand to me as I took that as a sign to shut up.

He rubbed his chin as he looked me up and down curiously. "So, you're telling me, if I let you stay in this competition amidst this scandal you would give it your all to win?" he said as I could only think to answer with a nod. "Curious. Of course, you'd be more anxious than ever with me walking in like this. It would be rude of me to not make up for that."

He looked at Brandon who looked at me as I looked back at him. I turned to Chef Roland confused until I realized he was unzipping his pants. Suddenly the thought of seeing this handsome older man reveal himself to me made me even more hot and bothered as well as terrified. He pulled his cock out of his pants and let me behold it in all its glory. He was longer than Brandon's, who was admittedly average-sized, but unlike Brandon, he was circumcised. He nodded for me to get to work as I turned one last time to Brandon who nodded with approval. He knew I needed this and to say no to what was apparently blackmail by a celebrity chef would be the end of my career as a professional cook as we knew it. I slowly approached Chef Roland and got down on my knees. I proceeded to slide his long shaft down my throat, letting his soft head ride along my tongue the whole way down. He tasted of salt and spices, much like the seafood, he was famous for making. His cock tasted delicious in my mouth. I rubbed my tongue along his shaft to feel all the new ridges and muscle that was different from Brandon's thicker meat.

Chef Roland rubbed his hands through my hair and like he really wanted me to know he enjoyed the experience. The only way I could think to tell him how much I enjoyed the taste of his cock was by going harder. He pushed his meat down my throat as his hands entangled themselves in my hair. I gagged and breathed heavily with each breath I could take. As I pulled away I let my tongue rub up against his shaft, feeling the throbbing veins as he was already feeling close. I grasped his testicles in my hand and massaged them gently as I pulled his cock out of my mouth so I could explore all sides of it with my tongue. I listened to him groan with pleasure as I stared up at him. It was so exciting to me that this famous face was looking down at me do my favorite thing next to cooking. I almost felt like this was a judgment I wanted his approval on more so than the competition.

He grabbed my shoulders and cupped my head as he thrusted his cock back into my mouth, his strength was something I've never experienced before. When Brandon mouth fucked me, he would never get aggressive. I kinda liked the aggression. I could tell I liked it because I felt myself touching my moist clit as he shoved himself deep into my mouth over and over again. I could see Brandon as he watched us and quietly stroked his cock. He was enjoying this. I never took him to be a cuck, but perhaps in the heat of a moment like this, he made a self-discovery. I smiled at him to let him know I was still enjoying it. I take another deep throat mouthful of Chef Roland's cock and suck it long and hard as I moan loudly now.

Suddenly the door opened again. I jumped where I was on my knees and gasped in surprise. It was Sous Chef Alex, Chef Roland's apprentice and one of the guest judges hosting the event. He had won this very competition less than five years ago and got the opportunity to apprentice under the famous chef. The two are seen together often now, so him being here isn't as surprising as it should have been. He looked at the two of us wide-eyed as Chef Roland gestured for him to make sure the door is locked. Alex nodded and pulled the door shut and fiddled with the bar lock until he was able to make sure it locked the door securely.

"We have ourselves a very eager competitor today Alex," Roland said to his apprentice. "She so far has been quite an impressive talent." They looked at each other almost like he knew something like this would happen or that it has happened before. Roland pulled out of me as I gasped for air and pushed me over towards Alex. "Show him what I mean, sweetheart."

I looked back up at Chef Roland in surprise. He wanted me to please his apprentice too? I looked over at Brandon unsure of what to say. Brandon simply approved with a steady nod as his eyes were transfixed on the situation unfolding. I looked up to Alex who smiled down at me. He was young like Brandon was, with a red-haired pretty boy face and clean complexion. I always found him to be cute, but never would I have thought we'd be in this position here. "Chef says you're good, I'm interested," he said to me with a chuckle on his face.

I breathed out and nodded as I watched him undo his

pants. Immediately I put my hands out to stop him so I could do it for him. He seemed to like that as I am quick to pull out his hard cock and clutch it in my hand. He was smaller than Roland's and Brandon's, though circumcised and arguably prettier than both based on appearance alone. I noticed how the shaft curved slightly to the right. His dark red pubic hair really helped set it apart from Brandon more so though. I breathed out and took his cock in my mouth. He had a bold savory taste to his dick as opposed to Chef Roland, his pre-cum already leaking onto my tongue like hot gravy. I proceeded to deep throat his dick, wanting to impress both of the accomplished chefs with my talent. I turned to Roland and took his dick in my hand and proceeded to jerk him off slowly while I let my tongue do the work on Alex. Roland chuckled with delight at my enthusiasm as he gestured for Brandon to walk over. I see Brandon approach me and I think nothing of it as I grab his hard cock and stroke him with my other hand.

I could feel the curve in Alex's shaft as it went down my throat. His skin was soft and smoother than Roland's rigid shaft but not as thick as Brandon's. He pushed down on my head with some moderate strength as he hard thrusted his dick down my throat to gag me. I cough some but keep sliding his cock in my mouth as my saliva has dressed it well. I pull out for a gasp of air before I turn and take Roland's rigid hard dick in my mouth for more exploration as I moved my hand to Alex's to take advantage of all the saliva making his dick wet and easy to jerk off.

"That's a good girl," Roland said as he petted my hair. "Share the love around, sweetheart."

I turned away and forced Brandon back down my throat as I revisited the familiarity of his salty-sweet hard cock. Brandon managed to gently pull me off both of the chefs as they started to completely undress themselves. My heart was racing fast with anticipation as I poured my love and dedication onto sucking Brandon's dick. I could tell whereas my Brandon was quiet and attentive, Roland was a groomer and Alex was an aggressor. I felt Alex as he grabbed me by my waist and forced me up onto my feet. "Get undressed, now," he said as he was breathing heavy already.

I watched both of the men standing there, stark naked and beautiful to behold. Chef Roland's body was more mature and thicker, yet still lined with muscle and overall healthy physique. Alex was skinnier and taller, with more hair on his body but not by much. He was also paler in complexion. I felt Brandon put his arms around me as he wanted to help undress me. He pulled my top and bra off as my breasts popped out and perked up for the men to behold. I was proud of my breasts, milky white and smooth with hard, erect nipples standing out. Brandon rubbed his hands down my firm stomach and over the curve of my abdomen as he pulled my bottoms down completely for the men to see my pretty, shaved, pink pussy. My thighs were already glistening from the amount of cum I had already emitted from enjoying their bodies. "Turn around and bend over," said Roland in a soft-spoken but commanding voice. "I want to see all you have to offer."

I obeyed as a good girl should and turned around for the chefs, showing them my tight, perfectly round and plump ass. I bent over some as I felt Alex grab at my ass cheeks hard. He dropped to his knees and immediately I could feel his mouth and tongue dip into my wet, exposed pussy. I moaned into Brandon as he helped me balance before I put his cock back in my mouth. Alex was aggressive as he licked my clit and pussy hole before going up over my taint and licking the rim of my asshole. I groaned some more as I felt my juices flowing from the amount of stimulation. Alex's fingers pushed into my hot pussy. "Jesus Christ, so fucking moist," he said to me. "You are a true slut, young lady, the best kind."

I shook in orgasm as I came all over Alex's fingers as he continued to eat my ass and finger me vigorously. I moaned again and again on Brandon's cock as he thrusted into my mouth. I felt Roland's heavy body push up against me as he wrapped his arms around me and felt my soft breasts and pinched my nipples as they hung out under me. Alex forcibly jerked my body back and forth on his tongue as he dipped into my asshole while his fingers curled inside of me and applying pressure to my moist walls. He fingered hard and fast as Roland practically milked me with his strong hands and I could feel Brandon throb in my mouth. I gasped for some air as I looked at each of them looming over me in enjoyment. "My turn again, sweetheart," said Roland as he held his long hard cock out for me. I licked my lips as I took him in again and rubbed Brandon with my fingers.

"Your pussy is quivering for more action," said Alex as he stood up and I felt him rub his cock over my wet clit. I shook with pleasure as he pushed a finger, already wet with my juices, into my ass at the same time he slid his cock inside me. He didn't push in as far as Brandon did due to his length but immediately, he began to shake my whole body with just the thrusting of his dick. His body slapped against my ass as he thrusted hard with several deep pushes that lingered for seconds on end. I moaned loudly onto Roland's cock as I felt Alex still manage to find my g-spot. He slapped my ass aggressively as I quivered and groaned. "The best kind of dirty slut, taking it like a champion!"

I was surprised at how aggressive and how loud he

was being but I did not care, his fucking was pure ecstasy as I found myself pushing against him just to try and match his speeds. I took in all of Roland's cock a few more times before pulling him out and sucking on his salty balls. His sweat was delicious as he smelled the manliest of the bunch. I was able to pick up more from loving on his cock now that he was naked. His scent of cigar and expensive cologne hit my nose at the same time as the savory taste of a delicious seafood platter. Meanwhile, Brandon got on his knees and rubbed my clit with his fingers in tandem with Alex's thrusting all while he sucked on my sensitive nipples with tinder kisses and light nibbling. Alex's nails dug into my ass cheeks as he fucked hard still with impressive stamina. I felt myself almost shout in pleasure on Roland's cock as my thighs were quivering from another orgasm.

"Turn her over, Alex," commanded Roland as I felt Alex pull out and as he lifted me by my legs into the air. I gasped with surprise as he dropped me on my ass and I stared up at the three men looming over me. Their silhouettes were an imposing view made from the bright fluorescence of the bathroom's lights. They created shadows that dropped across my body as I watched them each move into position. Roland first picked me up by my legs, taking a moment to rub his hands over the smoothness of my skin and adore my feet. I watched as Brandon and Alex whispered to each other for a moment before Brandon lifted me up by my arms. I wanted to speak and express my confusion but saw Alex as he made his way underneath me. "You know what is about to happen, sweetheart," Roland chuckled as he rubbed my legs gently.

Alex clasped his hands on my ass and spread my cheeks open. I could feel him rub his dick against it slowly as he lubricated with his saliva. Roland kept my legs spread as Alex pushed his cock slowly into my ass. I gasped with surprise and pleasure as I felt his smaller cock fill my tight hole perfectly. Of any of the three men to try it, I'm glad it was Alex. Roland watched me as my body shook and hopped on Alex's cock while he thrusted up into me. I looked up at Brandon who stood over me. He rubbed my cheeks before opening my mouth wide and thrusting his cock into my mouth. I moaned again with the pleasurable sensations.

I felt my pussy quiver as Alex pushed deep into my ass. Roland rubbed his strong hands over my clitoris as he watched, examining and enjoying every moment of the exhibitionism. He stroked his cock as he got down and dipped his tongue deep into my pussy. I moaned loudly onto Brandon's dick as I felt Roland tongue fuck my wet pussy, his licking met in rhythm with Alex's bold thrusts into my ass. I pushed myself back into the both of them just swaying my body in motion to theirs. The pleasure was overwhelming as my pussy clenched and my walls closed around Roland's tongue. I felt my body jerk as I orgasmed, hard. Roland pursed his lips onto my clitoris as I came. I could feel the roughness of his scruff against my bald pussy as it tickled and served to heightened the glorious sensations.

Brandon couldn't help himself as he began to thrust harder into my mouth. I gagged some feeling him slide down my throat. He grasped at my breasts and squeezed them softly. He pinched and pulled on my nipples in a milking motion. Alex lifted his body up to push me in the air so he could make longer and harder thrusts. Roland held me by my ankles so I could keep balance in the air with Alex fucking me from behind. Never before had I felt such a sensation as this. It was dirty, it was everything I wasn't. Except this time. Roland knew I was reveling in this moment and he seemed more than happy to oblige. He stood back up as his shadow draped over me again. I gasped through the thrusting of Brandon's cock to look at him as he took his dick and rubbed it against my moist lips.

I was moaning uncontrollably at this point as I felt Roland push his thick meat into my pussy. Though he didn't look a lot larger than Brandon, he sure felt larger. My walls stretched as I could feel his hard, rigid cock slide deep into me. His head pushed against my cervix as I found myself climaxing again just from the feeling of his cock pushing into me. He grasped my thighs with a strong gentleness that I wasn't entirely used to. He hoisted me up into him to relieve pressure off Alex as he proceeded to slide in and out of me, slow at first. I could feel my walls stretching and adjusting to the thickness of his cock as he pushed in and out slowly. He licked his thumb and proceeded to tease my clitoris even more as I began to writhe with pleasure.

Alex dug his face into my neck, licking my sweat and tasting my skin. He was forceful in his kissing as he pushed himself hard into my neck. I felt his hands move up my body to grasp my breasts and he squeezed them hard. I could feel the pressure of his fingers as they compressed my soft tissue and they immediately began to feel sore. Roland was commanding my pussy with harder thrusts now as his strong hands grasped my ass and Alex began to focus more on full filling his other senses with me. I could feel his dick throb in my ass as Roland squeezed it and he nibbled on my skin for a better taste of my body. Brandon pulled away as he rubbed his dick. I could tell he was beginning to climax but neither I nor he was ready for that.

Roland raised a brow and smirked as he pulled out and picked me up with ease. I felt my body arc up towards him as he grasped the back of my neck and kissed me hard and passionately. I was overwhelmed with both surprise and anxiety again at such an interaction with the famous chef, but I loved every second of it. He pulled away and smirked as he turned me around again. Alex stood up as Roland gestured for Brandon to lay down where he was laying. Brandon does so, of course, and I grasp his throbbing, erect cock. "Now ride your lover, sweetheart," Roland whispered into my ear. I felt a chill run down my body as he did so.

Brandon held my thighs as I spread open my pussy and slowly dropped down on his standing tall cock. It slid in with ease, my pussy having been stretched some by Roland's dick. Brandon groaned with pleasure still from feeling the inside of me. I proceeded to ride my body against him. Roland walked around me as Alex came up and slapped my ass. He pushed me onto Brandon as my breasts dangled in his face. He took advantage of the moment to lick on my nipples, which were sore and overly sensitive from Alex's rough handling. Meanwhile, I feel Alex preparing for a second round as he pushed himself back into my asshole. In this position, I could feel their dicks rubbing together inside my body through my thin wall. I push back against them both as they thrust against each other into me.

Roland took my head as moaned and groaned with pleasure and slowly pushed his cock into my mouth again. I could feel him throbbing as each of the men were close to climaxing. In unison they fucked me as I felt myself explode in another orgasm, practically screaming with the chef's cock in my mouth. My tongue ran over his ridges and explored his thick meat some more as I could feel him shake and groan. He grabbed my head and pushed it into his cock as I felt his hot liquid shoot down my throat. He unleashed a heavy load into my mouth as I drank it up happily. He tasted more of the salty and savory deliciousness I expected from his food. I rubbed his cock and balls with my hands to milk him dry, drinking up every last bit of his delicious cum.

Inside my pussy, I could feel Brandon erupt next. Watching me suck Roland dry sent him over the edge as he grabbed my breasts and thrusted more violently. I could feel him ejaculate inside me as his cum shot right onto my g-spot. I jumped with surprise pleasure from his cumming inside me. Alex groaned loudly and started saying 'yes' over and over again under his breath as he grasped my ass and fucked faster and faster. I could feel my ass get hot with his juices as he came inside me and it made his cock slide in and out faster and easier than before. I rode out the pleasurable feeling as I could feel my own cum seep over Brandon's dick.

The four of us were all out of breath as Roland was quick to get dressed. Alex redressed quickly as well as I laid on Brandon for a moment to catch my breath.

"That was beyond amazing, young lady," Chef Roland said. "Astounding work. If you cook half as good as you fuck, consider yourself in very good standing to win this whole competition."

I looked at him and gasped with excitement, having nearly forgotten where we were and why we were fucking in the first place. Alex stood next to him now as they're both fully dressed. "You will get a vote from me too," he said with a chuckle and a huff.

"We will head out one at a time, go ahead and get dressed," said Chef Roland. "No one will notice a thing."

Brandon and I both managed to stand as they slipped out one at a time. I watched in disbelief as I looked at my boyfriend with a need for confirmation. "Did that just happen?" I asked him with a hoarseness to my voice.

"Yeah, yeah that happened," he said with a laugh and nodding his head. "Come on beautiful, let's get you dressed. Time to slay the competition."

I nodded and looked at my clothes as I slowly started getting dressed. I laughed aloud to myself as he looked over to me. I turned to him with a devious smile on my face. "I think I already have."

A Blue Summer Dress

I see her sitting on the bus — a woman of my age. She is sitting on the aisle, her fellow traveler sitting next to her by the window. She has long hair — Blonde, or somewhat red, dressed in a long blue summer dress that suits her figure well. From the place where I am sitting, it is not completely visible; it seems that it is familiar to me.

We are approaching a bus stop. I get up well in time, two more stops to go so that I can walk forward a little. "Hey, hello Samantha, that was a while ago. Are you okay?" I ask her. She turns her head in surprise. "My name is not Samantha and I have no idea who you are. Ashamed and with (probably) a red head I look at her. "Oh, uh, sorry, I thought of you as a familiar person. Apologies for bothering you, I wish you a pleasant evening and please act as if I have not addressed you." Finally, I haven't seen Samantha in a while. I do know that she used to have a good figure with curves in your right places and that this woman could well be a somewhat more mature version of that.

She looks at her traveling companion and where I

would expect a shake of her head, she looks back at the woman with an astonishing look at first, which turns into a smile with an affirmative nod. The woman looks back at me with a serious look. "You looked at me for a Samantha; can I ask who that is?" "Samantha is a friend I have known from our childhood and have not seen in a long time. Perhaps that is why I thought you were so easy for her." "Yes, I realize that," she says. "And what would you have done if I were Samantha?" "Then I would ask you if you are okay and maybe try to arrange something to eat together again." She thinks for a moment. "Would she like that if you asked?" "Yes, I assume so. We have often eaten together in the past, went out and then went home together."

She looks again from the corner of her eye at her fellow traveler, who makes her eyes roll mockingly and quickly looks the other way to hold back her laughter. "Okay," the woman says now. "You have just spoken to me and I will soon forget the name Samantha, you have just asked me if I want to go out for dinner, I do not forget that." I look at her a little sheepishly and luckily for it too embarrassing she threatens to say, she continues. "My name is Kayla and if you stick to your plan, I would love to go out to dinner with you." Of course, I will not let myself be known and I confirm my offer and introduce myself as Jake. In the meantime, I sit down on the couch next to Kayla and meanwhile we talk about cows and calves. The other woman who has meanwhile introduced herself as Esther also talks along, while in the meantime, she still visibly enjoys with a big smile as a witness to the meeting between Kayla and me. After a few stops, she gets out of the car and wishes us a pleasant evening, where she can barely suppress a broad grin.

We eat a cozy little restaurant in the center, meanwhile talking about anything and everything. Out of the blue, Kayla asks if she really looks like my old girlfriend, or if I was just trying to decorate her a little. "Yes, you really look like it, even though after all these years I could have looked a little better out of my caps before I approached you." After the dessert, I beckon the waitress to order the last coffee and to settle the bill. Ask. Kayla looks at me doubtfully and asks me if my idea to go home also applies to her. I grab her both hands and look her in the eye. "This has nothing to do with a misunderstanding or a change of person, after this pleasant evening with such a beautiful woman and I would prefer nothing more," I say and immediately realize that it can seem a bit silly. "I live not far from here; you are more than welcome to come and have a drink." Together we walk through the city to her house.

When we arrive, we take off our coats and try to hang them on the same hook, bumping into each other. Kayla looks at me a bit surprised after a sigh of "Can we do this better at our age?" She comes close to me and kisses me full on my mouth. I open my mouth a little to sense how far she wants to go. She apparently feels this as an encouragement to let her tongue slip into my mouth. Here she finds mine, who eagerly takes up the challenge and in no time we are furiously kissing in the hall. My hands go down her back, where they find a good hold. I gently knead her nice firm buttocks, which she answers by moaning my tongue further into her mouth to suck in the pressure of her lips further. In the meantime, she presses her breasts firmly against me and I feel my pants getting tighter from the front.

"Come," she says. "Please come to the room, that's nicer than in this hall." We end up on the couch, where we crawl into each other in the cuddle corner and continue kissing. "That is a long time ago since I kissed so violently," I whisper as I release myself for a bite and a breath and then we move on. In the meantime, my hands are exploring and finding the outline of her breasts. Very firm and round, I guess cup C like that. I stroke them from below and let my fingers glide along the contours. A heavy moan and a bite in my lips encourage me to go up a little further and now support her breasts with my palms and continue to explore with my fingers. I let them run large circles, always smaller towards the nipples. Until I reach the nipples that have become hard and kneaded them gently between my thumbs and forefingers. In the meantime, I am almost kissed flat against the couch and I am looking with my hands for the straps to her dress and bra.

After making some space, a hand disappears in her cleavage en route to bypass the layers of clothing. Now I can grasp her full breasts with both hands and gently knead, meanwhile position her nipples in the direction of the index and middle fingers and gently squeeze them. She starts to pant and moan softly and let her head lean back so that we stop kissing. This allows me to kiss her in the neck and nibble her ear. I run my tongue over her earlobe and whisper softly "Hmm, you have wonderful breasts, do you like what I do with you?" A loud moan and a confirmation "Yes nice as you spoil my tits with your hands that makes me feel good for more desire." "Get those tasty prams out of you completely, and then I will suck you on your nipples if you like that." She turned and under seductive hip cradles overlooking her delicious ass, she slowly pulled her dress over her head. She dropped the dress on the couch and continued to yell at me with her shaking buttocks. "Turn around, I think I promised you something," I said, grabbing her by the hips and pulling slowly towards me. I gently park her on my lap and move my hands from her hips to her breasts. While I grab her full by her breasts, I take care of her nipples one by one with tongue and mouth and I press her breasts together so that I can take her nipples in my mouth at the same time. With great difficulty, I sabble on both at the same time, after which Kayla curves her back and starts writhing on my lap.

"You're not sneaking with your burdock against the bump in my pants, are you?" I tease her a bit. "Oooh you're cheating, I've already finished everything and you are completely dressed". I will not let myself be said and I pull my shirt over my head and throw it in the corner of the couch near her dress. "Well, now we are a bit the same, I believe. I can't reach the rest; there is a nice lady on my lap that I don't want to chase off. ""Still teasing, just stand up for a moment, then I'll let you know what's coming of it" as she stands and pulls my hands forward. I also stand and we automatically start looking for something again. I knead her buttocks in my hands again and press her against me. I feel her hands go to the edge of my pants and loosen my belt; the buttons must also believe in it. As my pants sink to the floor I feel a hand go over my hard pole to my balls. "Hmm, I'm going to have a good look at it," she says as she kneels. I can feel her tongue going up my balls and pole and she is challengingly turning around the top. She stops for a moment. "Hmm, shall I suck that nice bar of yours?" She asks me, looking horny. "Hmm, Hmm," is the only thing I can release. I feel a hand squeezing my balls together and a pair of soft, warm lips gliding over my glans. She takes it nice and far in her mouth and starts to blow with slow head movements.

I am slowly increasing my pace. I start to pant and moan, but she continues to enjoy. Before bubbling into cooking, I let myself fall back on the couch. "Are you leaving now for my treatment?" She asks me, teasingly? "Come here and I'll make up for it" while I grab her and let her sit on my chest. She looks a bit surprised at me, but while I grab her buttocks and make my head disappear between her legs. "Hey, I was busy" soon makes way for soft moaning and panting when I start to lick her gently.

Arriving at her clit, I start to pamper it with my tongue gently and gently suck on it. She starts to moan and grabs my head with two hands. She pulls me closer and moves her hips more intensively with my lick movements. "I want to enjoy it together," she says as she steps away from me and lies down in position 69 over me. I immediately continue to lick her clit while I feel her eagerly sucking mouth glide over my pole again. The harder I lick her, the harder she starts to blow me. In the meantime, I slide a finger over her asterisk. Encouraged by her reaction to that, I moisten my finger a little and let it disappear a little in her ass. Not too far, but I keep moving a bit. I feel a hand tightly around my balls and also a fingertip against and a little disappear into my anus. Apparently, she thinks, "What you can do I can do better". Moaning heavily I am now sucking, I feel then I will not keep this for long.

With a loud moan as a warning, I now bury my head between her legs and lick her clit whether my life depends on it. We both now feel it as a final and after a few moments licking and sucking it seems like we are both exploding. We both get ready to moan loudly; I spray Kayla's mouth completely full of my warm sperm, she lets her juices flow freely over my chin. She leaves my pole in her mouth and gently sucks me to the last drop and audibly enjoys it. After heavy aftershocks, we plump ourselves on the couch and lie down next to each other, our arms around each other. While we look at each other with satisfaction, I say a little earlier, "Wow, I have not come this intense in years. After this foreplay, I'm ready for a short break". Kayla nods affirmatively and asks if I also want something to drink.

"I'll do that for a while. I enjoyed your presentation so much that in return I am going to get a drink," I heard the voice of Esther, who apparently had been watching our party all the time around the corner of the doorway.

And that is how we sit on the couch, panting. I met Kayla on the bus this afternoon and after having eaten together, we ended up at her house together. At the door stands Esther, who had been introduced to me as Kayla's fellow traveler and who had left earlier than we were? I feel a little-watched, actually more of a surprise than of shame.

Esther explains to me that she and Kayla are roommates. They have bought a house together and they both have their own floor, they share the large living room and kitchen on the ground floor. When asked if they share more, Kayla laughs and says that they regularly lend each other a hand, such as getting a drink when the other person is just too busy. And if nobody were around that they still have each other. "Well, Kayla, tell me more than is good for our visitors, now you play innocently for a waitress and fill our glasses, leave the rough work to us". Kayla walks upstairs angrily, but I just see a twinkle in her eyes that makes me curious.

Esther and I crawl against each other again on the couch and with a little kissing and stroking the mood start to come in for the next round. I ask Esther if Kayla is really angry, the remark was quite blunt. "I'll take a look at how our waitress is doing," she says and the mocking tone gives me, even more, the idea that they are playing a game. I take my glass from the table and lean back on the couch; I can see what is about to happen as long as the ladies don't start arguing and the atmosphere changes. Then it gets dressed quickly and home I am scared. After a while, I hear rumble and laughter and the ladies come down the stairs. My mouth falls open in surprise.

Kayla and Esther come slowly down the stairs. Black patent leather shoes, dark stockings with suspenders and above both a black and white striped French maid suit. I have to think for a moment whether I am awake. To feel my spontaneous erection in any case or I just woke up spontaneously. "After I had promised Esther that she would not just pay for the heavy work, she was no longer angry with me, was Esther?" Kayla says, looking at Esther and making a kiss. "No, we are all friends again," is her reply and she answers the invitation with an exaggerated neat kiss on Kayla's mouth. After this, they clear the table and put down three new glasses of wine — all this with extensive voluptuous movements that give me the full view of the bodies of the ladies. "Yes, Mr. Jake, if everything is as desired, my colleague and I would like to withdraw," Esther asks without waiting for the answer.

The ladies walk to the center of the room, cradling their hip and start kissing each other and stroking that it is a sweet delight. They are clearly enjoying themselves and coming on their knees next to me on the couch so that they can continue the show right in front of me. I just assume that they can use an extra hand and I gently squeeze and massage the passing breasts and buttocks. Slowly the ladies start to get rid of their packages, only the heels, stockings and suspenders remain. They didn't have any panties.

The ladies now involve me in the game and offer me one by one of their breasts at my mouth and I eagerly kiss and lick them. I also take the hard nipples in my mouth to gently suck on them.

My hands now find two wet cats and they start to caress and massage them. Then the clit and I let a finger slide inside — as much as possible at the same time to put nobody behind. "Time for mouth work," Kayla whispers in my ear and the ladies sit down in front of the couch. Together they lick my jerk, along my pole, my balls and back. Certainly, because they keep looking at me, it makes me super horny. When I think it couldn't be better, I feel a few lips sliding over my glans and the ladies suck me into seventh heaven one by one. With pleasure, I let myself fall backwards on the couch so that my pole pours out of the mouth of one of the ladies and manages to prevent an orgasm. The ladies do not leave me alone; of course, they only allow themselves to be encouraged by changing positions. "Too late to flee, sir, if you sometimes intend to," Kayla says as she comes over my head with her pussy. I immediately start licking her and she moves with pleasure. In the meantime, Esther has gotten tight again on my pole. The ladies change positions once and while I lick Esther, Kayla sits down on my pole and lets him slide in and out of her pussy. I don't know how to keep this up for long. Kayla has got it too and helps me to pamper Esther. We are now licking her at the same time. I slide a finger in and Kayla takes care of her little star.

With two fingers and two tongues, Esther holds the kidney longer and starts moaning and shaking violently, before getting a hefty orgasm. After this, we will work on Kayla together with the same stereo treatment until she too is ready. Esther then lies on her stomach over the coffee table and Kayla climbs on top. I stand behind it and take them back one by one. I try to take it easy, which is not easy with this wonderful view. The ladies are still looking forward to it and both stimulate their clit so that they move considerably and the pace increases rapidly. The ladies come almost simultaneously and my seed also starts to boil.

I pull back my pole and walk around the table. Two mouths do their best to get me that far and it doesn't take long for me to cum. They manage to both sip up a jet of seed and keep it inside. They look at each other triumphantly and end up in a French kiss, with my seed slowly coming out of their mouths. Drop me on the couch and enjoy the view immensely. Esther and Kayla come hanging against me exhausted so that the three of us can quietly enjoy this wonderful free party.

"This was the ride for me, I could not have imagined this on the way this afternoon," I tell the ladies, but from their looks, I get the idea that it might well be a preconceived plan...

First Lesbian Sex

Kitty Donovan is the one professor that Meg admires the most. She's a sexy older woman who's brainy as well. Meg hears some gossip about Kitty but she refuses to join in. Kitty asks her to join her for week on a scientific research project and Meg is excited. But Meg doesn't know just how excited she's going to get or why. She has a discovery to make and Professor Kitty is going to help her make it.

College. Used to be cool, now it sucks. My best friend had dropped out, all of the boys were immature jocks, and now I'd just found out in my last class of the day, my favorite professor was leaving. Those three things would combine to make next trimester pure torture. I didn't really get along with that many of the other girls either. As a third year Undergraduate, I'd have to seriously consider where I did my last year.

It was depressing. I was too pretty to be intelligent. That's what everyone thought. I could dye my hair dark, put in colored lenses and wear conservative clothing, but it was hard to hide the biggest set of breasts in the school.

Add to that long legs, hips so curved they had a natural

sway and a mouth that always looked plump, and I had no hope of convincing anyone I was here because I wanted to be a scientist and discover cures for genetic diseases.

At least Joanne had understood when she was here. We'd both applied together from the same hometown, and we got to share a dorm. Now I was alone and, Kitty Donovan, my professor for Biology, has just announced she wouldn't be back after the break. That sucked because she was the only one here who gave me hope.

Kitty Donovan had a bangin' body and cover model looks. She was also brainy and had managed to get through all of the stereotyping and have a successful career where people took her seriously. I related to her, and I needed to talk with her before she went. Whether or not I continued my education depended on what she said.

I couldn't do this alone, and my parents were no help. My mother said there was a lot more money in doing pageants like she did and my father just kept lining up young millionaires so I never had to work to support myself.

Grammy had passed away last year, and she was the one who quietly pushed me to have ambition and to use my brain not my body to get what I wanted from life. She was right. I don't think I'd have gotten much if I'd had to be a natural flirt.

That didn't come easily to me despite my looks. I always felt awkward and a little scared with male attention. I'd seen and read my share of male porn and what they wanted to do with their hard cocks didn't encourage me to try sex anytime soon. I did have a bunch of girls I hung out with at lunch. Not best friends but we had a few laughs, and it beat eating alone and getting hit on every second.

Today they were talking about Kitty Flanagan leaving. I was trying not to sound too interested or seem too devastated.

"So, Kitty Donovan is leaving…" Sarah said to me as I sat down.

"I know. Maybe she's starting a family or something." I was trying to keep it neutral and just threw anything into the conversation ring. The girls all laughed.

"Yeah, good one, Meg. Funny." Sarah grinned at me and the others snickered.

"Funny? How? A lot of women take leave to start a family."

"A lot of women also have sex with men."

I was confused which must've shown on my face.

"You don't know, do you?" Sarah grinned harder.

"Know what?"

"Kitty…she likes pussies." Sarah exaggerated her whisper.

"Huh?" So she liked cats?

"Wow. I really have to spell it out for you. Do you live under a rock?"

They all laughed.

"Kitty Flanagan is a lesbian."

My face had an instant burn. I hadn't blushed over anything in ages. "Oh. Okay. Well, they can still be parents."

"You must be one too, are you? Sounds like you're defending them."

The group burst into laughter. I didn't want to stay and say nasty things about a woman I respected. What she did in her personal life was nothing to do with me and it certainly didn't make me think any less of her.

"Whatever, Sarah. I've got studying to do. I'll see you tomorrow." I walked off and headed for my dorm room across campus.

I saw Kitty walking towards the carpark trying to balance a box on top of another. "Here let me help." I grabbed the top box.

"Oh, Meg. Thanks so much. I was sure I'd be fine, but I didn't count on not being able to see where I was going."

"No problem, Miss Flanagan." We called her Kitty in class, but as she wasn't my teacher anymore, I wasn't sure what to call her, so I went with being polite.

"Call me Kitty. Thanks for the help. The Dean did offer, but I wasn't in the mood for taking things gracefully."

"I'll really miss you. It's hard getting anyone else to take me seriously around here."

"Don't you let them ruin your dreams, Meg. Go ahead and be the best scientist ever and find some cures. They're out there."

"I'll still work hard. It just gets me down sometimes."

Kitty piled her box into the back seat and then took the one I was holding. She opened her purse and pulled out a business card. My number is on this if you ever need to talk, or you need some extra tutoring.

I took the business card and smiled. "I really appreciate that. I'll try not to haunt you."

Kitty laughed and threw her head back. Her golden curls fell in disarray around her shoulders. She really was beautiful. "I have some time up my sleeve now anyway. Hey, you're interested in scientific research, aren't you?"

"Sure am."

"I never got to choose an intern for the break, I didn't see a point, but I'll be assisting some excellent scientists on Alzheimer's research. Interested?"

"Oh my God! That would be super awesome."

"Excellent. Are you able to stay over for a week? We'll come home on the weekend."

"Yes, of course. I've no other plans."

"Great. I'll pick you up here at seven in the morning."

"I really don't know how to thank you."

"Just work hard."

"I will." I ran to my room to pack every stitch of clothing I had. I had no clue where we were going, and I didn't care. I could call my parents in the morning.

****

"So, Meg. How did you enjoy your first day with your head over a microscope?"

"It was epic."

"You did very well. It's easy to tell you have a passion for it. I used to be like that."

"Don't you like it now?" I sipped my champagne. I wasn't really used such expensive alcohol to it, but it was the drink of choice for Kitty, and I wasn't going to argue. I felt very sophisticated at the ripe old age of twenty. I was certainly very relaxed.

Talking with another female with so much in common was amazing. She sure knew how to rock the casual playsuit she had changed into as well. The best I could do was yoga pants and crop top when she said to change into the most comfortable things you have.

After a bit of thought, Kitty answered my question. "I do like it still. But sometimes I yearn to be soaking it all up for the first time. When I see all of the young ones, like yourself, I get a little envious that I'm not making these wondrous discoveries for the first time again.

"I'm sure you'll make some very important discoveries in the future. You're not old."

"I'm not twenty either."

"Pffft...thirty is the new twenty."

"How about thirty-eight?"

"No way."

"Yes, way."

"Now you've left work, you'll have plenty of time to get into research."

She nodded and drank down the rest of her wine. "I'd like to make a huge discovery and tell all those prejudiced bastards to kiss my ass."

My eyes nearly popped out of my head. Then I just started laughing. I reached out for the bottle and filled up her glass. "You gotta fill me in. Promise I'll say nothing."

"Thanks to Dean Anderson and that uptight bitch on the parent committee, I was 'removed from the school for the safety of the students'." She shook her head, and I could see tears brimming in her eyes.

"What? How were you a danger?"

"It's a religious based school and they don't share my belief that everyone should be allowed to love any age-of-consent person we choose. Male or female."

I didn't mean to, but I know I went red. I know I didn't say much, but I was embarrassed about what had been said about her at school yesterday.

"What? You have the same views as them, don't you?"

"No. It isn't that. God, I've never thought that hard about what others do in their privates lives, some of the girls at school were talking about you."

"Go ahead, say it. I'm a freak because I like to have sex with women and not men."

"No, they never said that. They just mentioned it, that's all." I looked up from my embarrassed stare at the carpet and saw the tears rolling down Kitty's cheeks. I put down my glass and went and sat next to her. "To hell with them. It's none of their business. It doesn't worry me otherwise I'd never have come here." I put my arm around her.

"I guess not. It just that losing my job is the last straw."

"You'll find something better."

"Thanks."

She looked so soft and beautiful and so vulnerable I just wanted to kiss her pain away. Wait…I wanted to what? Kiss her? Wow. I'd never thought about kissing another woman before. I'd had some less than successful attempts with males who were smelly and had scratchy growth on their faces. What would the smooth skin and soft lips of another woman be like?

To hell with it, life was for the living, right?

"Teach me." I had an edge to my voice that I'd never heard before, and I realized, for the first time in the presence of another person, I was sexually aroused. I really was.

"What?" Kitty frowned at me and then she must've understood. "Oh, Meg. You don't have to make me feel better like that."

"I'm not trying to. I don't find males attractive. Maybe I'm meant to be with females. I want to try it and see."

"I'd be taking advantage of my position over you."

"What position? You're no longer my teacher, and I've asked you, not the other way around. I know what I'm doing. I must have this body for some reason other than being labeled a dumb blonde."

She reached out, and her touch thrilled me to the core. My cheek was on fire where she'd traced her fingers, and I knew this was the right thing to do.

"You're beautiful, Meg. Don't ever let anyone put you down for your looks. I can assure you brains come in all packages and so does the lack of them."

"Kiss me, Kitty. I've never had a sexual kiss I've enjoyed."

"Oh, Baby. Come here." She reached out both arms,

and I shimmied across the sofa, and she wrapped her legs and arms around me, stroking my hair. "You know this is not why I invited you here."

"I know. It's my idea. And I'm age of consent."

"Neither of us are beholding to anything after this one time. I'll never treat you any differently than I have today. I'm not up for a relationship, Meg. If you can't handle the feelings of attachment, it's best we don't get beyond a kiss."

"I'll be okay. I promise I won't flip out and become your stalker."

She guided my head to tilt my face up to hers. Those beautiful eyes and plush, red lips were so close. I breathed in the womanly scent of her, and I knew this was going to blow my mind. As if she had all the time in the world she touched her lips to mine, barely and then pulled away slightly again.

I sucked in a breath and my pulse went wild. My pussy ached in a way that I'd never, ever felt before. I followed her movement and caught her behind the head with my hand. She couldn't move away as I tasted those sexy lips with the tip of my tongue. She groaned and pursed her lips around the tip of my tongue and gently sucked.

Holy fuck, that was the hottest thing anyone had ever

done to me. My hand trembled as I placed it on the delicate skin of her inner thigh and caressed her. I pulled her in closer, and our lips met as our tongues collided in heat.

After a few minutes of frantic kissing, Kitty pulled away, and we leaned with our foreheads together.

Every part of me throbbed, and my panties were already wet. Why hadn't I discovered this before? I liked females, sexually. Not to say I wouldn't like a male if I met the right one. I agreed with Kitty that we should be able to enjoy both if we chose to.

"We've kissed. We can stop right now if you want to. There's no obligation to go any further." Kitty sat up and looked me in the eyes. "I'll never say anything to anyone. You've certainly given me the ego boost I needed. Thank you."

"I don't want to stop. I want you to make love to me. I want you to do whatever you want to me."

"God, Meg. Are you sure? I mean really sure?"

"No one is going to know. I'll be okay later. I promise. This might be the only chance I get with someone I truly trust to take care of me." That was so true it scared me.

I kissed Kitty then. I took her face in my hands and kissed her as passionately as I could. I couldn't let this chance go by. I just couldn't. After the kiss had left her groaning, I stood up and took off my clothes, every stitch. My heavy breasts ached, and my nipples were as hard as rocks.

I ran my hands over my hips and then over my well-cropped pussy. "You want me, Kitty, Don't you? You want to kiss my pussy?"

She looked at me like I was a Goddess. "Baby, I want you more than you can ever imagine. I want to hear you scream my name as you come."

"Do it then." I walked towards her. "Make me come." I'd never felt so brave. I knew that I wanted this, and nothing was going to stop me getting it. "Tell me how you want me."

"Sit on the edge of the sofa, feet up, I'll do the rest."

I sat with my ass on the edge, and I leaned back with my feet up on the sofa as well. Kitty took all her clothes off and knelt between my legs. "Relax and let it happen. If you feel like coming, let it happen. There can be much more later. The first one will be very fast."

She traced her fingers all around my pussy lips.

I groaned because that almost made me come.

"Meg. I have to ask you. Are you a virgin?"

"I've penetrated myself with masturbation, but no one else has ever come close. I always felt too scared a man would hurt too much."

"There will be a time when you'll want it to hurt, and that will intensify the pleasure but I promise I'll be as gentle as I can, and you must tell me if anything makes you uncomfortable or is painful. Everyone is different."

"I will. I promise."

"Good girl." She lowered herself and leveled her mouth at my pussy. "Your pussy smells so sweet. I bet it tastes that way. First, I'm going to tongue-fuck you. That won't be hard on your tight, little tunnel."

"Oh God. I'm almost coming hearing you talk about it."

"Baby, you've got a lot of coming to do yet." Kitty went down and slid her long tongue inside me.

I can't even begin to explain how that felt. It was as smooth as silk and as hot as lava. I never wanted that to stop. I gripped the sofa cushions, and my hips came up to meet her tongue strokes. "Oooohhh. Kitty, that's so fucking good…"

She just kept on going with her tongue and rested the pad of one finger over my throbbing clit. I almost ripped the sofa cover with my fingernails.

"Holy fuck, Holy fuck. Fuck, fuck, fuck." I'd lost all sense of decorum.

Ever so slowly she circled my hot clit with her fingertip and kept shoving her tongue deep inside me making gorgeous slurping noises as she did. When she used two fingers and rubbed them fast over my clit, I knew I was done in.

My whole body locked up for a few seconds, and the only noise I could make was a strangled noise in my throat. Kitty kept up her rhythm with her fingers and sank her tongue in and held it in there.

My orgasm broke like a bucking bronco, and I swear I gushed a river of come as I Kitty worked to drink and lap it all up. Over and over my cunt squeezed and let go, and I never thought I could ever experience anything as good as my first orgasm with another person.

As I slowly regained control of my body, Kitty, stopped what she was doing and smiled. "You taste like the sweetest nectar, baby girl."

"You really know what you're doing. Nothing can ever be as good as that."

"You're wrong. It can be better."

"No way. That was amazing."

"Now we get down to some real orgasms." She moved me so I was on my knees. "You have the sweetest looking ass, and your pussy is so tight and hot. I'm going to stretch you now. It'll feel good. I promise."

"I trust you."

"You're really wet, but for your first time being finger-fucked, I'm going to use some lube. I have some in my purse." She kissed my ass cheek and went to get the lube out of her purse. "I won't hurt you, not in a bad way."

"I'll start with one finger to spread some of this lube deep inside your cunt. I won't penetrate your ass, Okay?"

"Okay." My breathing was labored, and my breasts swung free below me.

The lube was a little cold, but the feeling of her long, slender finger inside me soon had me pushing back for more.

"I'm going for two fingers now, Baby. You'll begin to feel the stretch."

She was right. Two fingers did stretch me and the way she moved them inside me, pressing down on the lower wall inside me, and I felt something so intense about where she focused her fingertip pressure.

"This is you G-spot I'm rubbing inside you. It gives the most intense orgasms. Play with your clit if you want to. Just go easy, you don't want to come before you're getting finger-fucked properly."

"Shit, that feels so good. I can't believe I'm ready to come so soon again."

"The female body is able to orgasm unlimited times with the correct treatment. The only barrier is our minds."

"I don't doubt that the way I'm feeling." I touched my swollen clit and softly rubbed as Kitty moved her fingers in and out faster.

"Three now. This may hurt a little but rub your clit and it'll soon pass."

Wow. Three fingers stretching me was so good. Her fucking action became faster, and I heard her squirt more lubrication, and the cold shock made me tense up which made me really feel her three fingers inside me all at once.

"So good, Kitty. So fucking good. Keep going, keep fucking me."

"I'm going for four now, so rub that clitty hard. Push back for me, Meg. Push back and fuck my fingers."

I did what she said, and the burning stretch hurt, but it also felt amazing. I rubbed my clitty hard, and a lot of the lube had run down to it. That was fucking good, and it let me go faster and hard on my clit, and I pushed back and forward hard onto her four, bunched up fingers.

"Turn over, Meg. Squat onto my fingers, watch me fuck you."

I quickly changed position onto my feet and squatted deep onto her fingers. I fucked them hard, bouncing up and down as she held her hand still.

"God you're fucking beautiful, Meg. Yes, darlin' yes, fuck down hard onto my fingers, feel it. Come for me babe. Come hard."

I did. I couldn't stop myself. My clit action with her hard finger fucking brought me undone for the second time, and I cried out as the tremors overtook me and I pumped a second squirt of cum out of my pussy. I was so messy, and Kitty seemed to love that.

"Sweet Jesus, girl, you come so beautifully. I could spend a lifetime making you cum and never get tired of it."

"What about you? Do you want to cum?"

"You don't have to worry about me. This night is for

you."

"I want to make you cum. I want to know I can."

"You might not like the taste. Not everyone does."

"Let me try, Kitty. I don't know what to do really, but you'll help me won't you. You'll tell me where to touch you, where to lick you."

"If you really are sure."

"Open your legs for me, Kitty. I want to see what you look like." I moved to kneel on the floor, and Kitty sat on the sofa. I pressed her thighs apart, and the most gorgeous sight met my eyes. A deep raspberry pink edged her lips, and when I eased them apart, her inner lips and tiny clit were candy-pink.

"You're so pretty. I'm going to lick your sweet, pink clitty. I think I'll like it." I wasn't sure what to do, but I thought about what made me come when I played with my clit. I pointed my tongue out and flickered the tip of it over her clit as fast as I could. Kitty tensed up and moaned some curse words.

She clearly liked that. I kept tickling her swollen clit with my tongue until she began to writhe up and down and side to side. "Put your fingers in me. I need to feel your inside me."

I figured I didn't need to mess around with one or two fingers, and I sank three deep inside her and fucked her hard with them. I softened my tongue a little and lapped at her clit as hard as I could.

It seemed to take no time at all and Kitty's body began to vibrate, and she cried out my name as her hips arched up over and over and sank my fingers in harder.

"Oh fuck. I didn't mean to come yet. God…shit."

"I'm glad you came fast. It means I did it right." I slowly slid my fingers out of her when her cunt stopped clenching. She groaned as I licked her come off my fingers. "You taste like honey. I want to eat you out." I went straight down and began licking her juices from inside her and around her silky pussy lips.

"You're a fast learner."

"You're a good teacher." I finished cleaning her up and slid up beside her on the sofa, and we cuddled.

"I never thought this would happen." Kitty stroked my shoulder. "Are you cold, I can turn the heat up."

"I'm not cold, I'm just all shivery from the way I feel. If I'd known, a woman could be that good…"

"I'm glad you didn't. I'm honored to be the first."

"I can't think of anyone else I'd rather it be."

We shared a kiss that was deep, and I could taste myself on her mouth, and it felt right. I never wanted to stop kissing her. Once we finally stopped, I was horny as fuck again. I stroked her gorgeous breasts, and her nipples stood hard and proud. They were thick and long compared to mine.

I leaned in and sucked one into my mouth. Kitty arched her back, and I knew her nipples were one of her most sensitive places. I pulled and tweaked at the other one with my finger and sucked hard. Her groans were my reward. I went back up and kissed her on the lips.

"Sit cross-legged, facing me. Let's make each other come together."

I moved to copy the way she sat, and she reached over, squirted some lube on me and then herself and started to massage my clit. I massaged her in the exact same way. We moved together, what she did to me I mirrored back to her. It was sublime and perfect. We both began breathing a little heavier, and she kissed and nibbled at my lips, and I did the same to her.

Her finger work became faster and more centered at my clit, and I found the sweet spot of hers and rubbed it as she did mine. She kissed me again, and I couldn't get enough of her. I sucked her tongue into my mouth and let her do the same to mine.

"Meg, I'm going to come now. Are you ready too."

"Yes, fuck yes. I'm ready."

We locked our mouth together again and hammered our tongues and lips onto each other as our fingers worked hard to release the impending orgasm. When it happened, we both hit the jackpot, and we cried out into each other's mouth. Or bodies tensed and released together and we slowly, slowly came down from the climax.

"Wow. I mean just...wow." There were no words for that. I couldn't believe it was even real.

"I know. I've never had it so intense before." Kitty held me tight.

"We've got all week if you want." I know she said one time, but hell if I was missing out on this every night. I was sure we could do a whole lot more too. Somehow I knew we'd barely scraped the surface of pleasure we could give each other.

"Meg, I'm going to fuck you in every way I know possible this week."

"I'm going to learn how to make you come from across the room."

"They have things called clit buzzers for that. Remote

controlled." She smiled.

"Now you're talking. I bet there's plenty more we can do with toys."

"We could go a whole lifetime." She looked down her face reddening a little as she realized what she'd said.

"A lifetime suits me. Why don't we try it?"

"I'm so much older."

"Let's take it day by orgasmic day then."

"Perfect."

I held her, and I hoped we'd be together like this for a very long time to come.

An Existential Crisis

Ifelt I was going through an existential crisis. I had sex with Brett, typically for convenience, with Jasmine because I found it amusing, but also with occasional partners whose name I forgot the next day. One day I had the uncontrollable desire to go shopping in a sex shop, and although I turned red at the thought of entering one of those shops, in the end, I found the strength not only to go through the door but to buy the most risqué items. I also took some clearly marked articles for sadomasochism, thinking of using them with Freya or for some strange game with Jasmine.

As soon as I got home, I placed all my purchases in the lower drawer of the bedside table with maniacal care, taking stoic resistance in quelling my desire to try them immediately. I thought it would be easier to get them out during one of my sapphic trysts. So, I decided to go, after dinner, to one of the few places where I knew they could meet women who were not only not interested in men, but were open to casual relationships.

Over what I now usually wore as underwear, a classic black satin push-up bra and thong, I wore a green dress that Brett had recently bought me, and that had the great advantage of bringing out my meager figure.

I took the car to go to "L. Island", finding with a big stroke of luck, parking very close to the entrance of the restaurant. It was actually a lesbian club with almost no entry requirement, where the important thing was to have fun and not give too much spectacle.

Upon entering, I noticed sitting on the sidelines, a girl with long red hair, who was watching the clock and was probably looking for someone.

"Can I wait with you?" I asked, sitting next to her without giving her time to tell me no.

"Yes, no one will come," she replied, shrugging disconsolately.

"I'm Paige and you?"

"Lara and if you have some redheaded fetish please move along."

While not one of those beauties that make your head spin, she had a charm of her own. Her body was a mix of ingenuity and malice. She had curves at all the right places. I ordered a drink for both of us and noticed almost immediately that Lara was a girl with a very docile nature, eager to have not only a lesbian relationship but to be dominated, even though she didn't have the courage to ask.

"Listen, Lara, why don't you stop telling sitting here by

yourself and say what you want. If you like we can go to my place, where, and I will tell you this immediately, I'll put you in handcuffs and blindfold you to let you experience the pleasure I know that you have been waiting for."

"And if I want to stop?"

"You'll just have to say an agreed-upon safe word, for example, spaghetti, and I'll stop and let you go instantly."

"All right, let's go," she said, finishing off the drink she had left in one go.

The journey to my apartment was almost unreal, in total silence, with only the noise of traffic in the background. I was amazed by the ease with which I had made my 'conquest', but at the same time, I was afraid of overdoing it, being at the end a first date. Once we arrived, we took the elevator, and I immediately drew her to me to give her a long kiss, feeling at the same time the inviting ass.

"Will you hurt me?" she asked as I opened the front door.

"No, I will make you enjoy it," I replied, almost pushing her inside.

I immediately took her to the room where I ordered her

to take off her shirt, skirt, and shoes and then sit at the foot of the bed. While she was undressing, I took handcuffs and blindfolds, which I put on them as soon as she was ready.

"Tell me a little about who you were waiting for in that club," I asked as I took off my dress.

"Someone that I had met on a chat, and who wanted to do a threesome with her husband."

"So, you go with men too," I asked, taking the whip I had bought in the afternoon.

"Yes, but I don't like them very much, I was interested in her, her husband was more of a compromise."

I sat down beside her and started kissing her on the neck, making her feel my tongue on her lips every now and then.

"I think you give it up to anyone who asks you," I said pushing her on the bed. "But not because you're a slut, but because you don't even understand who you are and what you want."

I put my tongue into her mouth, where I found her ready to cling, and a hand inside her panties that were starting to get wet.

"Paige please," she began me the moment I took my

lips from hers.

"Shut up and open your legs, because now we start to do things seriously."

I started hitting her labia with the whip, but without any intention of hurting her, but only to excite her as much as possible, and then have an open field to play. Her breath began to gasp, and it became even more so after I slipped two fingers into her tight hole after moving her panties.

"Now turn around, but always keep your legs wide open," I ordered, giving her a kiss.

She obeyed and stood in the middle of the bed, while I took a leather paddle, which was also the result of my afternoon shopping.

"You have a splendid ass," I told her, slipping her panties into the groove of her buttocks, before giving her the first weak blow with the paddle.

Lara's backside had something magical about it, not only did she have perfect shapes that almost made Jasmine look ugly, but she had a look that said, "Take me and do what you want." I began to alternate strokes given with the paddle and simple spanking, kisses on the buttocks and light pressures made with a finger against her butt hole, making sure kiss it with her panties.

The girl's breathing became increasingly frantic, and I don't know how I managed not to give in to the temptation to wear a strap-on and sodomize her.

"How many men have you put it in your ass," I asked with some curiosity.

"So many, indeed too many, since no one has ever made me feel like you do now," she replied turning her head as if searching for my lips. I thought of that couple who had not shown up for the appointment, and who now could not enjoy Lara's graces. I slipped a hand into her hair before kissing her passionately, at the same time giving her some slaps on her butt.

"Now turn around and put your hands over your head," I ordered after unfastening her bra that rested on her wrists. As soon as Lara lay down as I ordered her, I resumed kissing her passionately, this time slapping her breasts, or squeezing her nipples. "I bet you look forward to it," I told her after nibbling her lips.

"Yes, but I'm going crazy with desire and I don't want you to stop."

In response, I slipped my hand into her panties, letting my fingers reach between her lips, which were so swollen and wet they almost sucked me in.

"Look how wet the slut is!" I said, taking off her panties, which were now only a hindrance "But don't worry, I know you can do better, just with the right stimuli."

Stimuli that were nothing more than new whip blows on that lake between her legs, half-fingers and fast tongue-strokes right in the middle of the gap, also given to savor the sweet taste of sin. Lara breathed with more and more anxiety, but I felt she was missing that something extra to reach the threshold of orgasm. So, I violently slipped four fingers into her, making her jump in pain.

"Ouch, you hurt me," she protested without much conviction.

"Shut up otherwise I'll use my whole hand," I replied almost contemptuously. "In fact, you know what I'm saying? That it is time for you to enjoy me, so get on all fours and lick my vag."

While Lara was on all fours, I took the blindfold from her eyes and slipped off my thong to settle comfortably on my knees, waiting for her attentions. The girl began to pass her tongue on my snatch too quickly, so much so that I had to resume it with some regret for her excessive ardor.

"What the fuck are you doing! Look, you're not licking an ice cream, but my vagina," I said to her with deep disappointment "So go slow and let me enjoy this or I'll spank you!"

"Can I ask you to lay down," she asked tenderly. "At least it's easier for me."

I contented myself by putting myself in the middle of the bed, and immediately afterward she crouched between my open legs to give me the pleasure I so much desired. Perhaps because it was more comfortable, or just because it was badly received earlier, Lara didn't throw herself like a madwoman on my pleasure center but licked it with grace and passion, I would dare to say with dedication, making me go wild too quickly for my liking.

"So, I like you, little bitch," I said almost crushing her head against my vagina. "Now that I want to fill your beautiful ass with something hard, but I want to enjoy myself while I make love to you."

I got out of the drawer of the bedside table a strap-on that I had bought in the afternoon, of the type that also had a small vibrating phallus to get into the vagina of the wearer. I stared at the prosthesis with frenzy, having only the only thought of bobbing Lara, who was on her side knowing what awaited her and was already crawling at the foot of the bed.

Despite my desires, before sodomizing the girl I

passed my tongue around her hole a little, also to give him a minimum of lubrication. However, when I heard Lara moaning, I could no longer resist, and after kneeling behind her, I sodomized her by slamming her half with a first lunge.

"Ah, you're hurting me too much," the girl exclaimed, almost trying to escape my grip.

"Shut up, I know you're already enjoying it." I replied, grabbing her hair "Tonight you go home with your ass broken, I just have to decide how much you want it."

I don't know if it was the little vibrator that I had in the vagina or the groans of pain and pleasure of Lara. What was certain was that I felt no fatigue despite the great movement I was doing, rather the more time passed, the more I had the uncontrollable desire to continue to sodomize that girl. Lara for her part not only did not complain in any way but had no restraint in expressing her pleasure, moaning incessantly.

"Tell me how much you like getting your ass touched," I said giving her a loud slap on a butt.

"I like getting touched by you." she replied turning his head towards me "And I don't care that my body is burning with desire, do what you want as long you let me enjoy it."

I gave two more lunges before pulling out of her ass and slipping it into her little hole, where it slid in smoothly. Lara was immediately overwhelmed by orgasm and she didn't even notice that I pulled back to sodomize her again, then alternating her pleasure doors. By now she could no longer utter a sentence of complete meaning due to her endless orgasm that ceased only when I threw her exhausted on the bed.

I took off the strap-on and then lay down and started masturbating using the biggest phallus, but soon Lara knelt between my legs to lick my crease. Her tongue seemed to want to fill every space between the phallus and my flesh, thus giving me such a sweet pleasure that I slowed my hands to be able to taste it longer. She understood what I was doing, so every now and then she used her tongue more slowly, while I masturbated with more frenzy. In the end, I too had the deserved orgasm that Lara drank to be able to then bring it to my mouth, in a long liberating kiss.

"Tell me where you live and I take you home," I asked as I released her hands.

She confessed to me that she still lived with her parents in an old building just outside the city center because she couldn't afford to live alone.

"Put these in, I ordered her giving her two small vaginal

balls. "I haven't finished having fun with you tonight."

"Please, my parents don't know," she tried to protest in a trembling voice.

"Don't they know you like to take it in the ass? Don't worry, I'm certainly not going to out you, just keep playing."

Quiet with my words, Lara slipped the two balls into her slit before slipping on her panties and skirt, without even imagining what was waiting for her. The only way to get to the car was to have real torture because after each step you had to stop to try to counteract the excitement that the balls gave you.

"Raise your skirt," I ordered her as soon as she got into the car "You won't want to stop me from playing with your flower."

"But I'll end up wetting it all up," she replied, knowing full well how pointless it was.

"Then pull your dress up to the waist," I said giving her a kiss. "And be careful not to leave your legs closed."

Lara obeyed me with her legs completely exposed and at my complete mercy, waiting for my next move. But I did nothing throughout the journey, except to occasionally give her a caress on her pool of moisture that was now a lake. Once I arrived in front of her door,

I had her skirt replaced, before entering the door and forcing her into a hidden corner of the basement. I made her bend forward and I raised her skirt, before slipping two fingers into her core.

"No, you will make me scream," this was an almost whispered plea, but already strangled by a faint moan of pleasure.

"And you don't scream," I replied, slipping a third finger into her.

I masturbated her furiously even using four fingers, constantly touching her vaginal balls with my fingertips. Lara bit her lips to keep from screaming, succeeding despite me using my fingers like a demon. I sodomized her with my thumb, finally giving her a violent and silent orgasm, which caused her legs to bend as she tried to stand up against a railing.

"See, it wasn't that hard to stay silent," I said, licking her juices from my fingers. "Now go home, but leave the balls in"

I left her my card hoping she would come looking for me again, and while I was returning home, I began to imagine what I could do to that girl so easy to subdue.

I was still very unsure of who I was and didn't know what I wanted but I knew I wanted her. It reminded me of that very first experience with Shannon all those many months ago. It was almost the anniversary of that meeting. The chance meeting with a woman that wasn't quite a whore like my friend had imagined.

Meeting Shannon was probably the best thing that had happened to me over those many months, she had seen a girl who didn't know what she was and taught her to be more than the lawyer I hoped to be. I was waiting for my life to start then only to find that my life would be much more than I could ever have imagined.

I still wasn't sure who I was supposed to be. I wasn't sure what kind of person I was going to become. However, for a moment, after meeting with Lara and unleashing the person that was within me dying to be free, I finally felt some kind of peace.

It had been a rough year, especially the blackmail situation with Finley. I hadn't wanted to deal with that situation and had begun to regret all of the many situations that I had found myself in, but there was something about all of the experiences that I had had up until that moment of the blackmail and the many moments since that had unleashed a part of me that I didn't know that I had inside.

Inside me was a girl that was learning to be more than the chaste woman I was brought up to be. I enjoyed lovers and they enjoyed being with me. I learned to harness an inner power within myself that could be very domineering at times. I enjoyed taking the lead and being with women, but I still also enjoyed my time with men and multiple partners.

What was I becoming, I didn't know. On that long ride home that night, I decided not to think much more about it. I knew that I was happy and content at that moment. I knew at that moment that I had finally done something that I really wanted. Something that fed the sexual beast within me. Was I a lesbian? I didn't know for sure.

My many times with Jasmine had confirmed that, and of course my night with the submissive Lara had definitely solidified that women had to have a place in my sexual life. I didn't know what my life would hold from this moment on. In my old life, before meeting Shannon, I had known what my life held for me. A job at a top, firm and probably one day married with kids. On this night, I didn't know for sure what life held for me.

I wasn't going to be able to focus on what my sexual life held for me for the next few months, I needed to study to take the bar and get started on realizing my full potential as a lawyer. I would probably continue my relationship with Brett, I didn't know what else to do in that regard. The relationship with Mr. Bauman had secured my place at the Bauman Law Firm and I worried, at least for now, what would become of me should that relationship cease.

However, our relationship wasn't satisfying me in the ways that I needed it to satisfy me. I needed more. Lara proved that. If none of the many other sexual experiences I had had weren't proof enough for me. What would I do then, I didn't know. I turned on the radio and began to take a drive. I could figure out exactly who I was later.

The bed was calling me and work would be the focus for the next few months anyway. I would figure out everything about myself later, tonight I would just revel in my satisfaction, hoping to one day meet Lara again. I turned on the highway and raised the volume on the radio.

"I'll worry about who I am tomorrow," I told myself. I would worry about that tomorrow.

His Cock Twitching in the Air

Keeping still, he let her stand by supporting her shoulders as she raised each foot to step out of the thin fabric. As he slipped them off her feet, the fabric dropped on him, and he could feel how damp they were. He moaned as he went to stand up, his cock twitching in the air.

Jade held her hand still as she slipped her stomach over the fabric of her bra. "Looks like this, too, has lace." She kept silent biting her lip as she rubbed her legs together; her squeezing ministrations bothering her even over the padding. Sliding his fingertips along the sides of the fabric where the clip was in the back. Sliding a few fingers under the knot, he rubbed the spot underneath it, "It seems a little tight right here; I bet a backrub will fix that though.

He smiled as she laughed lightly, "Yeah, I bet that's what you've got in mind."

He nodded, unsuccessfully trying to hide his grin, "I live to serve you, mistress."

Laughing, she chastised him, "You think you 're a clever fox; don't you," leaning towards him, she reached out her hand to grab his ass, "too bad I 'm going to have to punish you for that." Sliding her hand up her back, she slipped it under her hair and yanked him in a kiss, "After that, I think you 're going to have to give me something really good to get off my bra; any suggestions?"

"A delayed orgasm?"

Grinning, she leaned forward, her lips brushing her ear, "Who says you 're going to have one at all?" Sudden silence swept through him as he thought of her answer. "You know, I think I found out what it was going to be like; so, what do you think, do you still want to take off my bra?"

Kenzie looked carefully at her, "What did you decide?"

Smiling, she traced her finger down her bare chest and pinched one of her nipples, "It's a secret; guess you'll have to decide if it's worth it."

In reaction, he reached out his hands and turned her around to face the other way, and pushed her hair over her shoulder, "Can I touch you?"

Jade held still as she felt his fingers caress her back, "I suppose; since you asked politely." She jumped a little as he stepped forward, his cock hitting her ass. His fingers brushed down her shoulders and took the straps with them. He pressed his lips to her spine, leaning forward, as his fingers found the clasp. Unhooking her bra, he dropped it to the floor as he kissed the trail to her neck. He squeezed her boobs in his palms, his thumb and index finger slipping into place to taunt her nipples.

Kenzie squeezed the rough knuckles between his fingertips, grinning when he heard her groan. He took his time to play with her, listening to every sound that had escaped her mouth. Stepping up against her, he could feel his cock rubbing against the cleft of her ass, and he pulled her nipples out of her mouth, teasing her, "You really like it; don't you?"

When he let go, she turned in her arms and lifted her hand to knot in her hair as she led him to stand in front of the bed. Stepping forward, she forced him to take a step back and then yanked back to watch as he lost his balance and fell back to the bed as she let go.

Kenzie panicked as he began to fall, trying to get her to stand still, but unable to see he grabbed empty air pockets instead. Catching the firm mattress, he relaxed until he felt her climb up his body to sit on it.

Jade reached out her hands, stroking her skin reassuringly as she bent down to kiss him, "You really need to learn your place."

Looking up at her, he reached out and pulled her mouth back to his own, "Make me."

Snaking her hand through her hair, she pulled her head to one side and bent down, sinking her teeth into her exposed neck. Her pussy throbled as he whimpered, and she backed off crawling out of the bed, "Lay on the edge of the bed." She watched as he moved to his place thinking about all the things that she could have done when one particular idea took hold, "On your back, just like that, now put your hand on your cock." She continued, throwing a nearby towel at him, "Go ahead and put this under you, and then go back to the way you did.

She waited patiently as he did, as he had been told, and then walked over to the nightstand for the lubricant, "You 're going to play with me for fun." She opened the bottle, which she pressed to let the lubricant drip down. She grinned, laughing, as the cold lubricant poured over his soft, aching dick. Stepping forward, she wrapped her hand around him and led it up and down his shaft a few times, "And don't even think about getting off without my permission."

Jade sat down on a nearby chair, so she had a full view, "Faster. It's supposed to be a demonstration for me; remember?" she waited a few minutes and then gave her next order, "It looks like your other hand has nothing to do with me. Why don't you suck me on those fingers."

Kenzie could feel his cheeks red, but he gently lifted his fingers to his mouth, sucking two of them between his lips. Her pussy throbbled, and she was glad she thought she 'd put a towel down earlier. She watched as he screwed his mouth with his fingers, "They 're probably wet enough by now. Go on, I want to watch your smart mouth moan as your fingers slip into you." Her pussy muscles tightened as she watched her cheeks swell, and she lowered her fingers to her clit as she lowered her fingers to her ass. He slid his fingers into place, biting his lip as he moaned; his warm fingers slipped into it.

Kenzie looked up when he realized that she was entering the room; the blindfold prevented him from seeing what she had become. Tilting his head, he noticed that the clicking he heard was her heels making contact with the hardwood floor. He could almost picture the sway of her hips as she walked toward him.

She stopped six inches from him and looked down, admiring how beautiful he was; he was in a kneeling position, his ass balancing on his heels. Walking around him, she noticed that the light from the window hitting her hair made her look a brighter red than usual, falling down the taunt muscles of her back. Each hand clasped the elbow of the other arm, causing him to arch his back.

Bending down, she reached out her hand stroking her fingertips over her upper back, softly pushing her hair out of the way as she leaned in to whisper in her ear, "Do you know how hot you look waiting on your knees, your back arched, just begging me to touch you?"

Kenzie almost whimpered when he felt her hot breath on the side of his neck, "Would you like to know what I'm wearing?" Nodding his head, he could almost feel her laughing behind him as her nails dug into his face, "Then tell me." He was blindfolded and stopped as his fingers encircled his wrists. "You may move and touch, but you're not going to remove the blindfold. Do you understand that?"

Nodding, he replied, lowering his hand to help her hold on as he stood up, "Yes, mistress." Moving around, he reached out his hand unsure of where she was and met one of hers. The hand led his own to his body and then left, leaving his palm to rest on his bare thigh. Lifting his other hand, he soon found another hip; running down his fingers, he could feel a lace like a cloth under his fingers.

She grinned as she watched her fingers dance around the lace trying to remember all the things she owned. Reaching out, she caressed her cheek with the back of one of her fingers. As her finger passed over his lips, he opened them willingly sucking on her finger as she teased him, "If you're going to be quiet, I'll gag you and make sure you stay that way. Is that what you want?" Kenzie pulled her finger into his mouth sucking seductively as he shook his head. "Then you'd better do as I asked, right Kenzie," she replied, as her finger slipped out of his warm mouth.

"Yes, Mistress," he responded, already pushing his hands farther down the lace to see whether they were pants or cuffs.

"Why don't you start from the bottom and work your way up."

Nodding, he used her to hang on as he went down to his knees in front of her. Reaching his hand to her hip, he felt the strap of her shoes over a pair of stalks; pushing his hand back toward her feet, he could feel the high angle of her foot, "You 're wearing boots; denim, maybe three or four inches long, light blue."

She chuckled, chastising him gently, "You're only allowed to describe things as they feel; do you understand?" She waited for him to answer and looked at him warmly, "Would you like to take them away from me?" he nodded, respectfully waiting for her permission. "Even if it means using your wrist cuffs tonight?" she looked at him again and said, "Very well."

She waited while he unfastened the straps around her ankles, and then lifted each leg so that he could slip off the pair. Setting them aside, he turned back to her slipping his hands up her thighs as his cock twitched, "Your wearing stitches; the sexy stitched man." Moving up, he could feel the tight lace wrapping around the top of each stitch kept up by the clips of the trunk, "The trunk is mostly made of lace."

She chuckled softly as she watched his cock twitch beneath him, "And do you want the satisfaction of extracting it as well?"

"I do, Mistress."

"And if I add the ankle cuffs?" she grinned.

He nodded, knowing where the game was heading. He waited until she had given him permission, and then began to unclip the cranberry from the stockings. Slowly and sensually, he slid each of the stockings down her long legs and then returned to the cranberry belt. Slipping his fingers underneath to hold the straps he could feel underneath the thin silk fabric. Sliding the belt down her legs, he waited until she walked out of it and ran her hands up her now bare legs.

Gliding his fingers around his thighs, he slid his hands to his place, grabbing her ass, "Your panties are smooth and cool like silk." Turning his hands back around, he dipped his fingers between his legs, disappointed, noticing that she had closed her legs, giving him very little access. Rubbing his finger across her clit, she couldn't hide, he continued, "And they've got lace on the sides that hug your hips beautifully." Leaning forward, he pressed his lips to her hip and kissed her stomach; looking up, he kissed right underneath her underwear, "May I take those off Mistress?"

She smiled at his mischievousness and then bit her lip as her fingertips brushed over her clit again. Looking down at him, the black cloth that just covered his eyes, she could see the grin that scribbled across his face, "You may."

Sliding his fingers under the waistband, he began to pull them down slowly, revealing his skin to the room, and then stopped as he realized what she hadn't said, "What do I have to do for them?"

She smiled down at him and lifted her hand, caressing her lips with her finger, "How do you feel about being on your knees?" Kenzie felt his cheeks red as he sank, but turned back to his task.

She watched him slowly spread over his fingers for a minute, and then stood up to give him more lube. Sitting back down she didn't waste any time, her fingers going straight to her clit, "I didn't tell you that she could slow down." She watched as her submissive bit of his lip kept crying as he twisted his ass, his other hand running up and down his dick.

"Please," he begged, "Please, Mistress, let me come."

She moaned as she stroked her clit faster, "No." She looked annoyed as she realized he 'd slowed down again, "Faster."

Kenzie bit his lip as he hurried back, "Please, Mom."

Picking up her pace, his pleas only amplified her coming orgasm, "No! Now start."

"I can't. Please," he said, cut off as a long moan escaped him.

"Now," she moaned close to her orgasm, "come for me." Her head dropped back as she moaned about her hand. Kenzie, spurred on by her moans, arched off the bed, moaning as he walked across his stomach. She looked over at the bed as she came down and saw the gigantic mess he had made.

While cleaning up a little, she stood and walked over to the bed, letting her fingers trace through the bones of her hips, "Who do you belong to?"

He blushed, still keeping her fingertips over his chest, "You Beauty, only you ever." She grinned bending down to kiss him sweetly on her mouth.

Sliding her hand down her chest, she glided one of the cum trails with a finger and turned back to him, "It's a mess you've made."

"I 'm sorry about that."

Raising her hand, she brushed the back of her finger against her lips, "Test it." She watched as he paused to consider what she was saying, and then she opened her mouth wrapping her lips around her fingers and sucking it into her mouth. He raised his tongue slowly, running his finger up. When he had done, she took a towel that she used to clean up and gently wiped him back, "I want you to stand on the side of the bed and bend over."

She turned, walking back to the nightstand to pick up the things she 'd need, "I want your hands flat on that bed." By grabbing them, she turned back to him, glad he 'd listened to her. Sitting on the bed, she reached out to touch him, making him shiver as she took a nail down her spine. Sitting on the floor behind him, she picked up the ankle cuffs and then wrapped the first leather cuff around her ankle, fastening it to the other.

Standing up, she slid her hand up her back, forcing him to bend over the side of the bed even more. She lowered her hands and squeezed her ass, "You are mine and I'm going to do whatever I want you to do." Leaning over him, she brushed her teeth along her ear, "However, if there's something you 'd like me to do, your lips are free to beg me for whatever you need." She smiled as she saw the blush creeping up her cheeks as she turned away.

Standing directly behind him, she leaned over him teasing him as she brushed her pelvis across her ass, "Stay still." Lifting her hand, she took two of her fingers to her lips and wetted them between their bodies, aiming for his already slick entrance. Sliding her fingers inside of him, she felt her pussy throb as he tightened around her whimpering as she filled him, "Does that feel good?"

"Yes, Mistre-," he said, cut off as he moaned as she twisted her fingers inside of him, aiming for that particular spot inside of him. Reaching around him with her other hand, she let her fingers brush down her stomach as she reached for his cock.

She stroked him a few times, leaving her thumb running over her hair, and then gently spread her fingers inside of him, preparing him for something bigger, "Oh, baby, you feel so tight wrapped around my fingers." He whimpered, turning his face away from her blushing as he shifted his hips back, while trying to position himself so that his fingers can stimulate that spot inside him again.

Teasing him on her fingers, she reached out with her other hand for the little plug she was sitting next to him. Lifting the toy to his mouth, she twisted her fingers, burying them deep inside him, "Open your mouth." She waited for him to do so, and then shrugged the toy against his lips. Kenzie took the hint and slipped his mouth around the toy until it came down and the cold metal started to warm up inside his wet mouth.

Jade tapped the base against his lips, "Is it ready for me?" he nodded, opening his mouth as she pulled to the base, forced his lips to slide down the shape of the toy as it withdrew. Scissoring her fingers inside of him, she watched him cling to the bedsheets above him whimpering as she began to pull out. As her fingers began to slip out, she forced the end of the tapered tip into it, sliding the toy into it as she slipped her fingers out of it.

Grabbing a nearby towel, she cleaned her fingers and

saw him begin to move, putting out her hand to reassure him, "How does it feel?"

Kenzie tilted his hips and shook his ass back and forth a few times before looking at her voice, "A little strange."

Jade laughed to reach over so that she could tap the base a few times, "How is that?"

The tiny little taps vibrated inside him, making him shudder, "It's heavier than I'm used to, and it's really warm."

Sitting down on the bed beside him, she reached out to her hand, caressing his cheek as she turned him to look at her, "Didn't you get it all nice and warm?" His cheeks were red and he tried to turn away, but his mistress kept him still. Reaching over him, she pressed the toy against the base a little deeper inside of him, "Do you like how it feels inside of you?"

Kenzie bit his lip, nodding as the toy bumped into his walls. He stilled as he felt his fingers sweep softly across his lips, "It's the second widest set of three, but the other two are different shapes."

She smiled as he tilted his head waiting for her to continue, "The one is long and tapered, and the other is a little wider than the one near the base, but it has ridges all the way up." Thinking about how the one would feel pushed inside of him, he shuddered and moaned as the plug bumped that spot inside him again.

Grinning, she teased him, "Do you want to try one of the others?"

He blushed, biting his lip again as he said softly, "Maybe."

"And which one do you like the sound of?"

"The second one," Kenzie sighed.

Tilting her head up, she teased her finger through her hair, "Which one was that again?"

"The one who has the ridges," he said, almost muttering, leaning affectionately into her hand.

Reaching behind him she found the plug he was thinking about and turned her hand letting the cold tip trace up of his ribcage. She watched with curiosity as he shuddered and then pushed the edge down his jaw, "This one is a little too big for you to fully warm up with your mouth but I think it'll warm up just as easily inside your tight little butt." Kenzie shuddered as she slid the cold metal over his lips; this one seemed to be much colder than the first one.

"Of course, you should ask me to warm it up for you." Running her hand down his leg, she started to get up, "Why don't you get up on the bed for me. Face down, I suppose." Pushing the other stuff out of his way, she waited until he was relaxed and then climbed back up to the bed beside him, "Give me one of the pillows above you."

Kenzie raised his hand, trying to find the pillow she was

talking about, and finally finding it he reached back to hand it over to her. He stilled as he felt his fingers slipping under his waist to lift his hips out of his bed, so that he could slip the pillow under his stomach. Running her hands over her butt, she teasingly squeezed, "You are running out of time to beg the boy."

While wrapping her fingers around the plug that lay inside of him, she gently pulled it out, fascinated as it slid out of him, "Are you still wet enough or do I need to add more?" she saw him nodding and leaning forward, "Kenzie," chastised, biting into the top of his ass.

Whimpering, he reached out to knot his fingers in the sheets above him, "Yes, mistress."

Pulling back, she softly kissed the path to his neck, "Yeah what."

He groaned as he felt his tongue run up his back, "Yeah, I'm always a wet enough mistress."

Reaching for the lubricant, she poured a little bit down the tapered end of the new toy and then smoothed it down every ridge just enough to cover it, but not too warm it. Moving back to him, she spread her cheeks with her fingertips as she led the plug to the sheath, "You sure don't want to ask for a baby; it's terribly cold."

She grinned as he bit his lip and turned his head to face the other way. Kindly, she put the cold tip against his entrance and forced the giggling as he shuddered underneath her. She gave him a moment to get used to it, and then she moved the first ridge inside, "How does it feel?"

He bit his lip as he shuddered again; the plug had already begun to warm inside, however, "Cold."

Jade chuckled, holding her warm hand up this leg, "I meant the form."

He whimpered as another cold ridge came in, and he felt every increase and decrease as his body slid over the metal fitting to the form of the toy, "Ok."

Pushing another ridge inside of him, she said, "Just good?"

He bit his lip as the rounded ball moved deeper into him, "I can feel every ridge as it moves."

"Why do you really like that?"

Kenzie nodded leaning in her warm hand, "It feels," paused, moaned as she purposefully moved the plug inside, "very good."

Pushing on the toy, she teased his entrance with the last ball-like shape; the cold penetrating through the small bundle of nerves, "Saving the last of the biggest."

Kenzie kept whimpering as he felt the biggest ball-like shape sliding into him, "God, that's cold."

Jade giggled, gently pushing and pulling on the base of the plug so that it moved inside of him, "You're much tighter in this position. I wanted to make sure you'd feel every cold ridge as it slipped inside of you." He moaned holding on the sheets caught between his fingers as she slowly began to fuck him on it. "I'm going to make a bargain with you; my pussy is throbbing after playing with you, and if you can get me off in the next sixty seconds, I'm going to wrap my lips around that gorgeous cock of yours."

Less than a second after the words had come out of her mouth, he moved; jumping at her, he pulled her down to the bed and placed his hands between his thighs, stretching out his legs for better access. Reaching between her legs, he slid his fingers down her slit looking for her entrance; as he felt the dip, he pushed her to spear with two of his fingers as he leaned down.

Jade moaned, almost crying at her sudden attention as he licked his lips around her clit and sucked. Her head dropped back as he lapped his fingertips in and out of the sensitive nub with his tongue. She moaned whimpering as she grabbed the sheets above her head, but he didn't give up; she just kept sucking and licking that sensitive spot as she turned her fingers to hit that special spot inside her.

Shuddering Jade came around his fingers and cried out as his unrelenting mouth brought her to a second. Backing off, Kenzie rubbed her hands up her thighs, thinking about how much she'd love to be between them in a different way. She reached for him as she came down, drawing him into a hug. Smiling, she looked at him, "Do you really want my mouth on your cock tonight?"

Kenzie blushed, leaning toward her warmth, wishing he could see her, "You don't have to."

While lifting her hand, she affectionately caressed his cheek, "Lay down." She watched as he slowly walked back across the bed to lay down, "I will punish you if you move your hips; understand?"

He smiled, trying to get comfortable, "Yes mistress." Straddling his thighs, she leaned toward his throbbing cock, blowing cool air over his hot skin, causing him to shiver underneath her. Wrapping her lips around the head of her cock, she sniffed her head, sliding her lips down her shaft.

Kenzie moaned, raising his hips to the warmth that surrounded him. Whimpering, he grabbed the sheets as his nails crept into his hips, "I told you to keep going."

Holding her fingertips tight to his shoulders to prevent him from shifting, she slipped down his shaft a few times and pushed her tongue through the tip several times. After saying this three more times, she could feel her muscles contracting beneath her, "The only way you 're coming back is either inside me or around my cock. Do you understand?"

"Yes, Mistress," he said, the words coming out as a whimper as she flicked her tongue across the head of her cock.

"Good," sitting up, she ran her nails sensually up his

sides, "now which one do you choose?" he glanced in shock at his mistress. "Come on," she said to him, taking him to her lips and kissing him, she turned her head in her ear, whispering, "do you want to come inside of me or do you want me to bury my cock inside of you and fuck you until you shout my name?"

Kenzie blushed a deep crimson, but shyly opened his mouth, "Please," he hesitated, reaching for another kiss, "Fuck me." She moaned around his lips, her pussy dripping at the thought of getting inside, and she looked around for what she was doing with her strap-on. Grabbing it, she didn't waste any time sliding the straps up her thighs, and then tightened them. Moving back to her lover, she reached for his hair and yanked him in a melting kiss.

He could feel the hands of his mistress pawing against his body as she began to kiss his neck. He whimpered into her ear as her teeth crept into his shoulder, and the hand in his hair kept him still as she did with her body. Suddenly, he felt a hand curl around his own, and he felt that he was driven between their bodies, and then the gentle surprise, as she wrapped her hand around her cock and forced him to stroke her shaft.

Jade watched as he came up with the idea and began stroking her as he liked to be, and she leaned in her ear, moaning in encouragement. Lifting her hand to the palm of her cheek, she wrapped her mouth with her own, and began to push up her hand as she moaned around her mouth. Yanking his head back, she moaned in his ear, "I want to watch you wrap your lips around my cock baby. Can you do that for me?"

Kenzie kept going as her question sunk in, but he just smiled, blushing as he gave her space to lay down. He could hear her positioning herself, and he waited patiently for her to direct him. He felt a hand wrap around his own as she led him toward her cock. He bent over her lower legs and began to try to find her shaft with his mouth. He felt a hand brushing his hair as it reached behind softly leading him to her, and he deliberately stuck out his tongue licking over the top of the strap-on.

Opening his mouth, he let his lips slide down his head and, as the hand in his hair led him further down his shaft, he let his shaft penetrate his moist, wet mouth. The hand let up and began to roll up and down her shaft, paying attention to the sensitive head every time she needed to breathe. The hand came back after a few strokes, forcing him further down her cock, so that his head tickled his throat, and then he was free to go back to please her.

"You think you can take more?" Kenzie flushed, but grinned around the cock in his mouth. He could feel the hand squeezing in his hair and breathing as he was driven down again. He could feel his head at the entrance of his mouth, and yet his hand pulled him deeper down the pipe. He couldn't help but gag the moment he was forced to deepen his mistress' shaft. Just as soon as the hand had appeared, the hand was gone, and it was he who wanted to take the shaft down his throat. He could feel her hand caressing his cheek lovingly as she whispered encouragement to him.

She could tell when he was getting tired and wrapped his hand in his beard, leading him to his lips instead. Unable to take it any more, she sat down softly leading him to lie on his back. Reaching for a pillow, she said, "Lift your hips for me sweetie."

Kenzie, following what was being said, lifted his hips and relaxed in the soft pillow she placed under him. Looking around for the lubricant, she placed the bottle on her bed beside her and softly caressed her hands up her lover's thighs as she spread her legs. Reaching between them, she tapped the plug still stuck inside him and grinned as he moaned, "Please."

Gently caressing his hip with one hand, she used the other one to wrap her fingers around the base of the plug. Pulling back, he slipped the first ball with an audible pop. She looked up to see a handful of the sheets blushing. Pulling the toy out of it, each ridge sliding out one by one, and she watched as he bit his lip trying not to make a sound. Setting the toy aside, she reached for the lubricant and dripped a path down her shaft, which she used to smooth her other hand.

She kissed him leaning over him, bumping her lubricated cock against his ass. Reaching up, she gently slid her hand under her head to undo the blindfold, "Close your eyes." She waited a second and then removed the blindfold, "Let your eyes adjust for a second." Putting her hand in front of the light of the lamp she waited until she opened her eyes and adjusted until she moved her hand and let him adjust to that.

Kenzie looked up at her and said, "Thank you, lady."

Chuckling lightly, she looked down at him, "You're not supposed to thank me. I did it so I could look into your eyes as I bury my cock inside of you."

He flushed, his cheeks reddening, but he reached up and pulled her down for another hug, "Thank you."

Jade grinned and reached down between the two of them to put her cock at the entrance. Moving back to her husband, she looked into his eyes and then pressed forward, sinking a few inches of her shaft into his warmth. She gave him a moment to adapt and then pressed forward again, pushing another inch or two into his body.

He moaned as a few more inches filled him, and his eyes rolled back a little as her next thrust brushed up against the comfort spot inside of me. Gently, she pressed forward and buried the remaining inch of her shaft inside him. She noticed that he was breathing hard and still holding on for a moment to let him adjust as she caressed his body with her fingers, "Are you all right?"

Kenzie nodded his head, "Ok, I'm just going to fuck."

Jade nodded and moved to caress his hand, but her cock twitched inside of him, and she watched as he whimpered, his knuckles turning white around the sheets he kept on, "You need me to get really slow?"

He nodded, his body flushed as he moaned as she gently pulled out most of the way. Standing over him, she repositioned her hands on either side of his ribcage, so that she could hold on to him as she fucked him. Slowly she came forward and was rewarded with a long moan. Kindly, she began fucking him in long slow strokes, but she knew he wasn't going to last as long as he was vocal.

"Please," paused as another burst of pleasure shot through him, he could barely find his words, "please stop."

Jade instantly looked up at him, "What's wrong?" she watched as he flushed a deeper red and asked, "Do you need more lube?"

"I don't want to," he paused, embarrassed, "please, I want to be able to touch you."

She smiled sweetly and nodded to understand what he wasn't saying; gently she scooted back and watched her cock slip from inside. Moving back, she sat back, crossed her legs, and then looked up, motioning for him to join her, "Come here."

Kenzie blushed a little more as he realised what she wanted him to do; climbing up to her lap, he leaned up on his knees, holding onto her shoulders for stability. Reaching around him, Jade placed her hard cock at his entrance and put her hands on his shoulders, gently pulling him down. He could feel her shaft impaling him as he lowered himself, and he moaned as he felt his hands wrap around his back. When he sank all the way down, he leaned down kissing his mistress as he felt one of his hands slide up his upper back, the other finding his place on his lower back right above his ass.

Lifting up, he began to fuck on her cock, bouncing up and down on her hard shaft, moaning every time it filled him. He could feel her hold on him passionately as he got closer to the edge, "Mistress ..."

She knotted her hand in her hair and yanked him down to kiss her, "Shh." She paused, kissing him, "Cum for my child."

It was hard to bounce up and down her shaft while kissing her, but he tried, moaning around her mouth as she brought her hips up to meet her. Lifting up, he bent down, kissing her harshly, just as she moved her hips forward, grinding her cock into him. Kenzie moaned upward as his head fell back as he came between them, and his cum covered his stomach. Sinking back down on her hard shaft, he shuddered the sensation under her hands.

"Put your legs around me." He whimpered as every movement pushed the cock in his ass, but he obeyed her. He felt her hand behind his head, and then, as she leaned forward, laid it down with her on top, her strap-on still buried in the hilt inside. Moving so that she could touch his lips, she kissed him for a long time and passionately took her time to savour the taste of him. He reached up and wrapped his arms around her slender body as he was lost in the moment. Gently pulling out of him, she caressed his thighs to reassure him. Loosening the straps, she put the strap on the other side of the bed, and then leaned over him, kissing him sweetly.

Jade shifted to lie beside him and placed her arms around him just as another post orgasm shudder passed through him, "When you're ready, I'm going to take a bath and pamper you."

He turned to look at her and said, "Thank you."

She leaned to kiss him, "Your welcome sweetheart."

"This is the ..."

Jade glanced at him, remembering that he had

reddened again, "What?"

"This is a lot stronger than usual."

She smiled at him, running his fingers through his long red hair, "I noticed. There's nothing I like more than to make love to your child."

He turned in her arms smiling as he snuggled against her warm body, "I love you."

She could feel him vibrating against her, "I love you too Kenz," wrapping her arms tightly around his thin body.

The Most Wonderful Weekend

Lynn and I had the most wonderful weekend recently. A friend of ours stopped over and we all had a night that we would never forget.

Marie is a long-time friend of mine. She is short, voluptuous and very bi. She and I have flirted for ages and she always thought Lynn was cute as well. Over the years, they grew closer as friends and both commented on how pretty the other was (have I mentioned that Lynn was bi too?).

Well, Marie called me up and said she wanted to come over and have some fun. I was definitely interested and a quick phone call on the cell confirmed that Lynn was looking forward to it as well.

Marie came over late in the evening and we sat around talking and relaxing in each other's company and friendship. We made converastion with Anne (our roommate) and her date for a while and Lynn went up to bed feeling suddenly tired. Marie and I conversed longer with them to seem social as we stole feels of each other's body when nobody was looking. At one moment, I went to 'help her find something to drink' in the kitchen, which gave us the opportunity to kiss and fondle each other's bodies until we were breathless and determined to continue it upstairs.

She commented that she was Lynn's guest and was 'going to mess with her for going to bed early'. I decided I was going to take a shower because I wanted to be fresh and ready for whatever the night held. I squeezed and rubbed her ass down the hallway to our bedroom and opened it. Lynn laid beneath the blankets, but was definitely not asleep because she turned around, as Marie climbed into bed with her, and started kissing Marie. I took that as a positive sign, so I smiled at both women and stepped out for a very quick shower.

After my shower and when I went back into the hallway, I could hear soft liquid sounds and sighs from behind the door. I went into the dark room and turned the lights on to find both girls sitting on the bed. Lynn was naked behind Marie who was exposed from the waist up, her large breasts hung enticingly with erect nipples. They were smiling up at me as Lynn was kissing her neck and stroking her body.

My clothes were quickly shed (put on just in case the roomies were in the hall) and I smiled at Lynn before I kissed Marie passionately on the lips. I felt her heat burn into my mouth before I moved down to her ample bosom and started sucking her breasts, nibbling and chewing on those large nipples. Marie stroked my head. I noticed she still had her jeans on under the blanket, and of course, they had to go.

Marie understood where my hands were heading. She leaned into Lynn and lifted her hips to help me ease them off of her. After pulling her jeans off, I sidled up to Marie's left, putting her between Lynn and myself. As they went back to kissing and fondling each other, I feasted on her breasts, kissing up and down her side. My hands stroked up and down her thighs, then pulled them apart to expose her freshly-shaved pussy.

I lightly touched her there and felt her breath catch in anticipation, which fueled me to spread her wide open. She was so wet that her juices freely flowed from her, coating my fingers as they started circling and stroking her clit. Lynn slid down and worked her way down Marie's body to suck on her other breast.

I moved down as well to get a better angle so I could slide a finger deep into Marie, whose groan was so deep and heart-felt that I knew she hadn't been touched that way in a very long time. Her body clenched my finger and her hips worked up and down to get every bit of feeling from that initial penetration.

I was at the bottom of the bed, licking her legs and pushing a second finger deep inside ... then I curled them and stroked her special spot; Marie's hips jumped off the bed and her eyes were as big as saucers when she gasped from pure pleasure. I looked at her through my long braids and said, "I told you that I learned some new tricks ..."

By this time, Lynn had come to the bottom of the bed as well and was kissing Marie's thighs as my fingers were doing their magic. Inch by inch, her kisses went up from the knee, slowly and achingly working their way toward her wet, hot, dripping pussy. Lightning seemed to shoot through Marie's body when her lips made contact with Marie's clit, Lynn's tongue was flicking and fluttering all over her sensitive button. Combined with the thrusting, twisting and polyrhythmic motions of my fingers, she was constantly stimulated, never knowing how I was going to move next as I twisted deep inside her.

Marie started coming very hard, bouncing up and playing with her nipples while grabbing at Lynn's head. The wetness created by them poured over my probing fingers, soaking my entire hand which made my fingers move in and out of her nearly frictionless. Her G-spot was my target and I hit it with every finger flick, twist and combination that I could manage from that position, and she loved every second of the pleasure. Lynn excused herself to go to the bathroom and I slid down between her legs to press my tongue flat against her clit. I licked up and down her pussy, making a point to rub the entire raspy flat of my tongue against her clit.

My fingers rubbed her pussy all over, spreading her lips apart and moving her juices from her clit down to her pretty, puckered asshole. Marie moaned even louder at the contact and pushed against my probing hand.

Marie's fingers gripped my head, pulling me deeper to tongue every bit of her. Her thighs moved back and forth, alternating between clasping my face when she comes to spreading wide to give more access for my probing hand. Lynn returned to the room and watched us for a few moments while rubbing my shoulders, asking me how good the flavor was. My response was rather muffled by Marie's thighs, but I gave an extra flick to Marie's G-Spot with my fingertips and made her come as punctuation to my statement. Lynn went up to Marie's side and they continued to kiss.

Marie turned to Lynn and started sucking her breasts, making Lynn press against her talented mouth and moan softly. I reached up between Lynn's legs with my other hand, spread her legs and eased a finger into her tight, wet hole. She sighed with pleasure as her liquid heat engulfed my finger while I worked my way deeper into her wetness. The unique pleasure of having fingers moving in and out of two women simultaneously can only be described best by experiencing it ... I became so erect that my shorts were tight and my cock was begging to be released.

I reveled in the incredible sensations I received from these two lovely women and received such incredible sensations from both at the same time: texture, reaction to penetration, the unique way they orgasm, the wetness caused by stroking their spots ...

I began pleasing both women at the same time, but in different ways and speeds. Lynn had a little to drink, which makes her extra-tight, so I used one finger inside her, pushing deep because she loves penetration and the occasionally rubbing of her G-spot. With Marie, I had two fingers inside her super-wet pussy, twisting them inside of her like the twin serpents on a caduceus. I flicked her G-spot often, giving her a continual set of orgasms while she feasted upon Lynn's breasts and body.

Some time later, Marie wanted to return the favor to Lynn and flipped over on the bed to dive, face-first, between her thighs. Marie's tongue made contact almost immediately. Lynn's back arched and the first of many pleasure shocks rippled through her body.

I stood, watching the pleasure before me: Lynn's writhing body being devoured by a voracious Marie, who was feasting as though it was the first meal to a starving woman. Marie's big, round ass was up in the air, looking delicious and inviting. I was torn as to whether I should slide my super-hard cock inside her or play with her a bit longer. Lynn looked up at me and mouthed what I understood as 'Get her'.

I blew Lynn a kiss, which was lasciviuosly returned, then went down and kissed a wet trail down Marie's back and over her big pretty ass. I massaged her round curves, knowing that she loved her ass being played with as much as I loved doing it. I spread her cheeks, then started licking her tight little hole with vigor. I put a hand on each cheek to keep her spread wide and pushed my tongue deep inside. She clenched my probing, twisting muscle and bucked up at my face to get even more inside her sensitive orifice.

I moved a hand down to rub her clit, driving her delirious with pleasure as she was making Lynn. My tongue went in and out of her over and over, stretching her slightly and getting her even wetter than before . Eventually, I pulled my tongue out of her ass and licked her pussy for a long time, feeling her juices all over my face. I slapped her ass intermittently to make her grind against my mouth.

Lynn was in a near-state of delirium from how Marie was eating her. The slurps and sucks from between her legs meshed perfectly with the gasps and moans that came from her lips. Shetried to pull away but Marie locked her arms around her thighs and held her down for a bit longer. Lynn, knowing she was at the mercy of a woman whose pleasuring would not be denied, fell back on the bed, fully enraptured by the delights of Marie's lips and tongue.

I eased a finger into Marie's wet, relaxed ass and two fingers into her even wetter pussy, pumping her with long deep strokes. Both of her tight holes milked my fingers as though they were my cock, and I could imagine how my swelled member would feel penetrating her luscious body. I was relishing the fantasy of filling her with my manhood so much that I was intensely throbbing and started to leak precum, causing a spot on my shorts to spread.

I was broken from my fantasizing by the very loud and strong orgasm she had. Marie's body clamped down hard on my fingers and she twirled her hips around, grinding against me to savor every moment. After catching her breath, Marie released my fingers from her grasp and Lynn from her hands, then slid up the bed to her. I watched them kiss and lick each other's faces, then I seized the opportunity to lick Lynn's open wet pussy, tonguing her up and down with gusto.

My hands held her hips down and kept her bucking down slightly so I could see over her sexy body. Both women were adoring each other's faces, necks and shoulders with kisses and licks. The sight of that passion made me even harder than before. I pressed against the bed with every movement on the mattress, causing achingly sweet vibrations through my shaft and balls.

I licked and sucked the sweet nectar from her body for so long that she got overly sensitive and started pulling away, but I had no intentions of letting go. Both women started pushing me away, and once the seal of my mouth on her clit was broken, she scooted back to catch her breath and calm down a little.

I moved up to where I was earlier, putting Marie right in the middle. Lynn and I began kissing her all over again, sucking her hard nipples, our teasing tongues against each other. Lynn and I reached between Marie's legs, getting our fingers wet all over again, then slid them inside her simultaneously. Our fingers pumped and twisted inside her at two completely different cadences until she came hard and shuddered.

As I moved up to kiss her again, my erection pressed into her thigh. She grasped it, then stroked it passionately, massaging my entire length. I looked into her eyes and calmly asked, 'Find something you like?'

She replied, 'Oh hells yea!' with a throaty giggle. I leaned over to kiss Lynn and she said, 'It was time to take care of me'.

Marie told her to jump on me and ride, but Lynn told

her she could go first, which surprised Marie and made her blush a little. Lynn excused herself to the bathroom again and I moved to the middle of the bed, legs spread with my manhood standing at full attention, eager with anticipation and curious as to what the rest of the night would have in store for us.

Marie got between my legs, grasped my shaft and began sucking me so hard and hungrily that she had to be satisfying a long-wanted craving. Her hot, sucking mouth swallowed about half of me from the moment my swelled head passed her moist, hungry lips. I could feel her tongue slither up and down my manhood when she would pull me from her mouth then swirl over the head as she pulled me back in deep. She felt so good sucking and licking my cock that I nearly lost it. I had to throw my head back and moan loudly for some time; the sounds of my own pleasure combined with Marie's wet, sucking mouth helped bring me back down from the clouds and help calm myself.

Lynn returned to the room and was greeted to see Marie's mouth stuffed full of my engorged cock, yet plenty still for her hand to play with. As she was sucking me deep, she started stroking me at the same time, rocking up and down as she pleasured my entire length. All the rocking made her ass point up in the air, inviting Lynn for some more foreplay.

Lynn looked up at me and we winked at each other before her face disappeared down between Marie's cheeks. I know she must have been licking furiously because Marie was moaning and groaning loudly, even with her mouth full of me. She reached below to rub the area below my balls, which made me pour more precum into her mouth; she sucked harder to make sure every drop was pulled into her hungry, gulping mouth.

After she decided she had to be filled, she sat up and Lynn was licking and kissing her back and neck. I sat up and kissed her breasts, squeezing them until she moaned. I put my arms about her and pulled her down on top of me so she could straddle my body and get ready for me. After she put the condom on, she got up on top and started to line herself up to slide down my shaft .

The look of bliss on her face when my head eased inside her was beautiful. We both moaned deeply at the heat when I started to enter. Lynn watched from the foot of the bed, seeing Marie slide farther down on me. The initial look of bliss turned into the sexiest look. When she pushed down, impaling herself with my shaft, I must have gotten in much farther than she expected because her eyes slid into the back of her head and her mouth opened wide in pleasure as my entire length inside her. That image of pure eroticism will forever be burned into my mind.

Soon Marie started moving up and down on me, faster and faster, gripping me from root to tip. I had to think of something—anything—other than how good she felt or I wasn't going to last but a minute more. I held her hips and told her to grind on me so she could feel me pulse deep inside her. She was loving the twisting actions of our bodies being so close—pelvis grinding to pelvis—then I started to flex my cock inside her, thickening the shaft, enlarging my head and making it twitch back and forth, pressed all the way inside her. That feeling caused her to make the sexy moan for me again. I knew she was enjoying herself, so I sat back and enjoyed the ride.

Marie started bouncing, twisting and turning so happily on my shaft. I squeezed her breasts and tugged her nipples every time I could to send shocks down to her clit. We started thrusting harder and harder, faster and faster until she came so massively that she jumped up from me and just stood there, shivering and shuddering from the power of her climax. Lynn and I held onto her for a few moments while the shaking stopped and she laid back on the bed with us.

After she'd calmed down a bit, she told Lynn to climb aboard me. Lynn straddled me and was about to ease down, but I stopped her and told Marie to put my cock inside Lynn. She loves to watch and the thought of getting to penetrate Lynn with my cock was too delicious to pass up. She gave me a Cheshire Cat smile, grabbed my shaft from the root, then put my head right against her wet opening, then pushed us against each other until I popped inside. She stayed right between our legs, watching happily at the sight of my shaft disappearing and reappearing into Lynn's dripping wet pussy.

I felt Marie's hands on my legs and I asked if she was enjoying the show. She was devouring every movement with her eyes, moaning softly in agreement as she watched Lynn's sinuous motions while she rode me. I decided to spice things up a touch and told Lynn to turn around so her back was facing me and she could lean back on my chest. Lynn started turning around, keeping me inside her as she bounced up and down.

When she had completely turned around with her back facing me, I helped her ease down so her back lay against my chest. This exposed her to Marie, who got to see Lynn's pussy up close; her hard, throbbing clit and lips spread wide open with my thick, hard cock stuffed deep into her tight hole. Marie crawled closer and sucked on Lynn's clit, which made her come instantly. Lynn's juices flowed even more freely over me and she had a string of multiple orgasms without pause.

Marie's hands proved to be as agile as her mouth. Her fingers start playing over Lynn's spread lips and my balls while she continued to suck and lick Lynn senseless. Marie grabbed the exposed part of my shaft, working it up and down to increase the sensation. I played with Lynn's upper body as Marie pleasured below. I kissed and nibbled on her neck as I played with her breasts, squeezing her breasts hard the way she loves it, and used that as leverage to push her body even deeper on my shaft. Between Marie's mouth and my cock, Lynn came so hard and squeezed me so tightly that I popped out! Marie noticed with surprise that Lynn's orgasm was so intense that she had squeezed the condom right off me!

After Lynn climbed off, Marie got on all fours and started kissing her again. I got behind Marie and rubbed my head against her wet slit that parted her lips then thrust deep inside. Burying half of my shaft inside her with the first push, she groaned and pushed back against me to fully sheathe myself inside her hot, slippery body. Her hips moved up and down so forcefully that my manhood felt as though it was on a rollercoaster. She asked—no, demanded—that I fuck her hard, so I grabbed her hips and started thrusting deep and hard into her. I slapped her ass and thrust deep, flexing and swelling my cock so hard that she cried out in pleasure.

Lynn lay beside us kissing Marie and playing with her large, swaying breasts. I massaged and slapped her large, round cheeks to the coos of her delight. My only goal at that moment was to give her every bit of pleasure she wanted, what she deserved and what she desired. I kept up my pounding and thrusting until she collapsed on the bed, shuddering uncontrollably in pleasure. Lynn pulled Marie's head to her bosom and caressed her as she pulled off out my cock and panted over and over, grinning about how much she was overstimulated.

My manhood—thick, swollen, pulsing and glistening—stood above the women with a drive to pleasure and be pleasured. Lynn lay back with open legs and beckoned for me to come closer. I nestled between her thighs and leaned back to give Marie the view of me as I slowly slid my entire length inside Lynn's hot, wet pussy. Her back arched and I could feel her every inner muscle stretch to accomodate my thrusting. We groaned and hissed when I fully sheathed myself inside her hungry, twisting body. I leaned forward and put an arm around both women to pull them together so we could all have a hot, threeway kiss. Our lips and tongues met and we all moaned as we tasted and savored the flavors on our mouths, which got us even hotter from the thrillingly unique contact.

Nearly breathless from the kiss, we all leaned back for a moment. Lynn looked at me, begging me to give it to her hard and deep. With renewed resolve, I pinned her to the bed, fully in control and thrust inside her with long, twisting strokes. Lynn mewed at me, completely enraptured by my forcefulness and threw her pelvis at me with every deep stroke, sucking me even deeper into her tight wetness. Marie stroked my arm as she murmured words of encouragement.

"Fuck her good ... give it all to her ... make her come hard ... fuck her harder, harder, harder! Yes baby, it looks so good watching you fuck her like that ... I love watching you two fuck ..."

Lynn's hot, tight, wet body wriggled around my cock, combined with Marie's hot body pressing up against us, and soon it became too hot for me to handle. Amidst the sounds of Lynn's orgasms, Marie's erotic words and the slick liquid sounds of our bodies moving against each other, I pulled my manhood from Lynn's body. Blast after blast of my seed flew from my cock, arcing over her body as though it were launched from a cannon. I gasped uncontrollably and had to brace myself against the wall for support while my orgasm ripped through my entire being.

I purred like a great cat and smiled down at the incredible women before me. I was even more pleased and surprised when they began feeding drops of my seed to each other with their fingertips, smiling and winking at me the entire time. With my composure somewhat regained, I leaned down to kiss both women and told them how much I enjoyed myself.

Marie said that it was better than she imagined it would be. We'd been together a long time before and she knew I'd be incredible, but she was so surprised at how good Lynn was in bed. We looked at Lynn to ask her how she enjoyed it, but all she could do was smile and giggle. I held both women against me in a very loving embrace, kissed them both and simultaneously wished for the moment to never end, hoping the next time would be even better.

Sex with Laila

Sex with Laila was constantly cluttered, but if she whispered in my ear mid-fuck that she'd be needing my bum next, my pussy clutched itself about her hand so hard that I anticipated her knuckles to emerge bruised. I rode my orgasm as my fingers dropped in her raven-black hair while colors collided in my mind. My muscles clung to the rhythm of her past strokes inside me. Then she surprised me by turning me on my belly, spread my buttocks bare and, apparently, made it all hers. I'd assumed she meant the next time she fucked me. I simply hadn't presumed this to happen so fast.

Laila was responsible in the bedroom and from the kitchen, the two rooms of the apartment were where I was only required to function, to take any initiative. I'd been a sous-chef at great in both areas, but my delight always came. I was well-fed and filled, alive on a diet of finely spiced dishes along with my girlfriend's yummy golden-brown fingers buried deep in my cunt at fixed intervals. Thus far, she'd only teasingly ventured from the path to my bum.

She covered my naked body, her tender flesh molding

right into mine.

"Your butt is mine tonight," she hissed in my ear, while still spreading my legs along with her knee. I wondered what she meant with 'mine'? Can she just lick it, finger it maybe or rely on other items? Or was all that combined? I knew better than to ask. From the sack, Laila did all the talking.

When she pushed himself away from my ear, her tight nipples grazed the skin on the spine. They swirled patterns on my backbone together until they rested on my bum cheeks. As Laila rubbed one nipple along my crack, and despite the banging orgasm she'd just delivered, I felt myself become moist.

This was sex. This was breaking boundaries.

I gasped as she parted my lips and enabled her nipple to research a little farther. I envisioned how the caramel of her skin and the dark chocolate of her nipple contrasted with the creamy whiteness of my butt. The tender side of her rigid bud was sufficient to create my asshole pucker with expectation and, first time or not, to give her unlimited access into the unchartered land my bum represented.

Not that she'd ever ask. Laila appropriated things. She took them within the dynamic of their sex life. They just belonged to her since our affair wasn't complex. She fucked me and I cummed.

Her hair tickled my spine and no matter having no ability to see her, I could readily envision the smirk edging her mouth round. I'd seen it usually with a couple of Laila's fingers deep within me, to understand its details. Two nice lines bracketed her lips as they bulged upward. Intensity burned in her eyes as she got off from my joy and from the way I constantly, so readily, acquiesced.

She slipped one hand between my thighs, beneath my pelvis and discovered my clit, which was a bit sensitive in the preceding round. Her nipple softly probed my crack while she circled a finger across my clit. Once, twice, only enough to create arousal and I needed more before she needed to focus and yank at my rear door.

Laila was an expert at driving me mad and, so, she made me want to do things I never knew existed until me fulfilled me with a fist in my cunt and had metallic clamps on my nipples.

The area smelled of climaxes needed and climaxes still to be bestowed. The heady perfume of expectation mixed with filthy delight.

On the way up from teasing my clit, she coated her hands with the juices dripping from my cunt. She traced a line from my pussy to my asshole and substituted her nipple with a wet fingertip. After dark, I felt like all of me jumped into Laila with no exceptions.

She could do anything she wanted. Have me, cuff me, whip me. This feeling multiplied when she circled the meaty portion of her finger along my delicate passing. If Laila would ask me to wed her, this is how she would do it. By asserting me hers, totally.

She entered slowly, allowing my body to adapt to the newness of what she'd been doing. My clit throbbed and my muscles tensed because the trick slipped in, invasive but proficient in precisely the exact same moment. I had no reference point because of this particular, no previous experience to quantify those sensations. My asshole sucked in her finger as she pried deeper. I could hear her pant because she worked me with enthusiasm, which was pretty much the basis of Laila.

Before moving deeper, she pulled and began the round movement again, drawing perfect circles round my rim. Laila understood me well, as though she would read my physique. She knew I'd be needing more shortly. I wanted her.

This time, she pushed her finger in and out, only far enough to get me to gasp for air each time she exited her finger, extending my asshole. Without a doubt she was imagining it for what was to come.

"I knew you would like this," she said, her voice falling to that minimal enthrall reserved for kinky actions. "You're all mine now, babe." As if I was not already. "Mine," she repeated and enlarged me further by adding a different finger.

I yelped, unprepared for the filling feeling, the depth of two hands I could readily take in my cunt—a fist was more common—unexpected me from the trunk. However, I took it just like the fantastic woman she knew I was.

Juices leaked out of my pussy, bathing my clit in wetness. I wanted to reach out and rub on it, to increase the pleasure that was suffering from behind, but I was reluctant to proceed. Together with two fingers, Laila had me trapped with her fist under her, the only way she desired.

She explored me farther, twisting her palms whenever she stroked me indoors. Bright white celebrities popped up on the rear of my own eye-lids since I buried my head to the pillow. Certainly, I couldn't orgasm simply with her hands in my ass. In any event, I was sure Laila wouldn't let me. She was nowhere near done.

Stroking turned into thrusting while I sensed her hair dancing on my bum cheeks. I envisioned the white globes of my bum being parted with her palms, her brooding brown eyes staring down at me there. No one had seen me the manner Laila had and that I was pretty certain nobody ever would.

Her own hair slipped down my buttocks as she reduced herself and put a tender kiss near the very top of my crack. It stood out in stark contrast to how she was managing my asshole, ravaging it with her palms in an increasingly merciless speed. If my hands was anywhere close to my clit, it'd have been enough to propel me to a different star-shattering orgasm.

She trailed a course of moist kisses along my bum cheek and, if reaching the very top of its curve, piece of my flesh. Another jolt ripped through my body, tightening my muscles and left me breathless. My pussy appeared like mad, roaring for focus, screaming for release.

I panted into the cushion as she withdrew her hands, leaving my bum wanting more.

"On all fours," she commanded.

Controlled and arousals coursed through my bloodstream as I exposed my pussy into the musky air of the bedroom. I depended in my hands and knees and, looking back through my arms, hunted for her eyes. I discovered shadow, pure sexual appetite mixed with all the will to own. To get and to give.

She reached for the bedside table where we kept our toys and observed how, from underneath handcuffs and blindfolds, she unearthed a dildo. Perhaps not the greatest one she possessed, but not the tiniest one either.

My throat went dry at the sight of it. Two palms appeared like nothing when it was compared with this sexy pink silicone penis she was going to negotiate into my virgin ass. Fortunately, she grabbed a bottle of lube behind her and applied it to my back, then went on her way back into deflowering me once and for all.

She squirted a generous amount of lube onto the toy,

never caring that half of it spilled on the sheets and along with her knees. I saw her bring the dildo into my bum and I shut my eyes. I had no other choice than to distribute myself to the darkness. She rubbed the cock along my crack, spreading the lube around. My muscles packed once I felt the trick at my rim, not probing just yet, only familiarizing itself, like mentioning a polite hello before raiding me.

I braced myself for effect, however, rather than easing it softly into my buttocks, Laila rammed it into my soaking, wet pussy first, coaxing a loud shout from my neck. My cunt responded immediately, lugging itself around the slick shaft of this toy, sucking it in. My clit stood to attention, but Laila was too smart to attend it. I wasn't in the border yet, I was not prepared to beg for launch. And she hadn't fucked my ass nonetheless.

She kept slamming the penis into me and I bucked down tough, my thigh muscles straining to grab it as I possibly could. When my groans betrayed my degree of enthusiasm, she retracted and dragged the tip up to my crack.

I exhaled and tried to unwind, my body trapped in a frenzy of lust and sweltering desire. I wanted it today. Wanted her to grope my bum. Wanted her to take me. She put a sexy hand on my bum cheek while she placed the dildo near my asshole. It was hot and slick with my juices, prepared to slide in. My asshole automatically enlarged at its signature, bidding it a warm welcome.

The head disappeared inside me. Readily, my entire body parting for Laila. I heard her gasp with wonder. She has to have been soaking wet, her juices dripped onto the elaborate silk sheets she returned after her final trip to Morocco. The dildo filled me to the brim because she pushed deeper. Never in my life had I felt owned, therefore enslaved to a single individual, therefore at her will.

As she began to slide the toy with slow continuous movements, my asshole relaxed, extending and contracting across the girth of the dildo. A simmering fire stirred within my stomach, setting off explosions in my blood. The celebrities in my eye-lids returned and now they blazed brightly, absorbing me. My mind spun through nothingness and what as my own entire body gave up itself for the new intrusion since I surrendered.

"Touch yourself," Laila said, her voice more than tones of pure bliss, syllables strung together by the fire.

Her command stunned me, but I figured that in alerting me to her will from how she was doing, it was a way she'd never explored before. I had fantasized about it a lot. She'd be amazing herself, too.

I let myself slide onto my shoulders, pushed my ass up high and shifted my weight to one side. My fingers couldn't reach my engorged clit fast enough. My cunt flexed about nothing while I whined to this aching bud between my thighs. Laila maneuvered the dildo with much more conviction, out and in again, reluctantly driving me to new heights, taking more of me. I felt her free handshake my butt cheek as I trembled towards orgasm.

Galaxies collapsed from the shadow in the front of the eyes, giving way to torrents of color. I saw the cherry, exactly the identical color as the dildo Laila was using to fuck me. I saw myself willing, loving it into rainbows as warmth catapulted through me.

Feverishly, I worked my clit, rubbing it back and forth with my finger. The feeling of being filled to the brim paired together with the immediate stimulation of my clit, was just like exploding into paradise.

"Come on, baby," Laila hoarse voice moaned. "Come now."

She knew I'd been waiting for her to allow me. I always did.

The muscles across my asshole began contracting on their own volition, pulsing electrical sparks of pleasure throughout my bones. I discovered that perfect place in my clit, the one which is always very sensitive, and I stroked myself into an obliterating orgasm. I arrived afterward, for Laila, full of her love for me, also along with a hot pink dildo.

Gradually, she withdrew the toy. Talking about everything, I fell onto the mattress. My whole body throbbed and I knew, in that instant, there wasn't anything that I wouldn't do to her. At least not at both designated chambers of the house, where she was the manager of mine.

She poured her sexy body, covering my sweat-soaked back together with her torso, her wrists caressing every piece of the skin they could touch. As much as I adored the orgasm, the only physical piece, this component, the bewitching wake up, was consistently the ideal.

"I adore you," she explained, her voice back to normal. Her mouth was buried in my hair, her breath hardly reaching my ear. I knew I didn't need to mention it back. I'd just revealed my love for her.

Her nipples, stiff as marbles, poked onto my shoulder muscles. "The next time," she continued. "I believe I will use the strap on." She slithered up my body until her lips found my ear. "I believe you're prepared for dual penetration." She bit my ear lobe before relaxing her muscles, her entire body moving soft along me.

I could barely wait.

That was the very first time my girlfriend maintained my bum and took me all. I have enjoyed it ever since.

My First Threesome

There I was nude as the day I was born, flat on my stomach, on a lumpy mattress in a grade B hotel just above Vienna where all my family was summering at. I was then 18, a "rising senior" in high school, so I worked in my first job in the summer. I had come with my manager on this spot in the gift shop where I was working. We had some pretty sweet yet furtive sex in the store closet a couple of times.

Nevertheless, he needed, and I wanted, a more detailed encounter, so one evening he proposed that I meet him and we'd go to a hotel. He said he'd tell his wife that he'd play poker with his best friend, Bill, and a few other guys. I didn't know much about it, but Bob, Joe and I were involved in a sex threesome.

The first time we stepped into the motel room was when I saw Bill first. He was lying in his boxers on the bed and a blue and red checked work-shirt with stickers above the sleeves, one with the shop tag where he worked as the parts manager, and the other with the word "Bill." Once he got up, he had to be six foot three inches tall, which is damn big compared to my five feet six. Joe immediately put his arms around my middle and whispered in my ear, "This is my friend. We can have a great time with him, but if you're scared, I'm going to understand..." I guess I'm the opposite type of gal. If I haven't already told you, I have a hit of the same, the proof of which is that I went first with Joe to the motel room, trusting him on the basis of absolute zero facts.

Joe made the presentation, holding me up against him all the while. I could see his cock growing up while his chest was rubbing against my back and my sensitive breasts were cupped and his fingers massaged it. Joe kept licking my neck and behind my ears as we stood there. They just melted away if I had any doubts and my nipples got even more rigid and stiffly erect!

Joe kind of moved me over to the bed across the dingy carpet. "Oh, oh, what a beautiful little thing," Joe said. He reached out, and cupped my cheek. "Girl," he said, "you're going to love this. With that, Joe started to tug on my blouse, pulling it over my head. I was wearing a simple white bra that stuck out from my summer-tan skin. I unbuttoned my shorts and let them drop to the floor. I reached down and tugged my underwear off my thighs, stepping out of them, too. I was there, my pussy, adorned with a small reddish-brown pig thatched me. He reached out one big hand and pinched a nipple, sending a thrill through my body and allowing my inner juices to start lubricating my cunt. Bill rolled out of his top and quickly pulled his boxers beneath his knees. His dick, still semi-hard, was very,

very wide and only partially covered the most significant set of balls I've ever seen. He stared at my sex, opened his eyes, and, stroking his cock, crawled to the foot of the tallest, his mass eclipsing the light overhead. Joe, lying next to me, started sucking on one breast, nibbling on my nipple while Bill stretched out and spreading my cunt lips with the fingertips of one hand. He ran up and down my slit with one fat finger, brushing my clit gently and then driving it deep inside me. When he started to fuck me, I shut my eyes with satisfaction. I heard the bed shifting and the ancient springs squeaking, when Bill again changed his position.

Bill then began pushing his dick inside me. I shut my eyes as the wondrous sensations from my vulva reached out. Bill pushed a bit, then pulled back and grunted. Adjusting himself, bending over, putting his hands on either side of me to sit on the pillow, he said, "Damn, she's close," grunting as he attempted to force his penis inside me. I placed my hands on both sides of his arms and I tried to pull him to me. Even though he was a stranger, I just wanted the cock inside of me. It's hard to explain but while it's kind of terrifying to see such a big organ, it's also exciting.

I felt his rod digging into me, his fat head cracking my mouth. Just how it feels is hard to describe but it was b-i-g. Finally, it slid out and his hands dropped in between our bellies with his dick. "Fuck!" he yelled. I sighed in sorrow.

He tried again, taking his dick in hand, and it fell out once more before he could enter my gushing pussy. I forced my hips greedy as he tried again and he slipped out again, this time his giant member slid down over my little asshole and between my ass cheeks. "Ohhhhhh," I grumbled in disappointment.

Bill rose up and kneeled down between my thighs. He said, "Hey, Joe, you've got to put me in while I'm bending forward and driving...." Since that time, I've had several three-somes and the guys always seemed phobic of touching each other (although they love to see the gals making out). Yet Joe went out, bringing Bill's organ into his left hand without hesitation, and pouring in a few times while Bill laughed.

Bill then bent over me, leaning on either side of my head with his large frame on his shoulders. I saw Joe moving Bill's cock's head into my opening, peering down between my breasts, over my stomach. It didn't fit very comfortably in yet, so Joe said, "Wait for a moment," and turned around behind Bill. Joe reached between the big thighs of Bill and kind of cupped in his palm the pulsing organ, bringing it back to me. Bill's big balls sat on his arm and bounced out a few as Bill leaned back.

Bill's big cock started sliding back into me this time. The massive head fell inside me first. Joe stepped back a bit from Bill's dick, and they pushed back together. Then... it slid into me and filled me like no other cock before. When Bills dick plunged deep, deep, deeper into my oh-so-willing cunt, Joe took his hand off.

I sensed Bill's massive stomach settling upon me as his dick bottomed in me. I remember his big, cum-heavy balls rolling against my anus as his cock settled in me, moving its hips in small circles about. While he was as far as he could go, I was trying to flex my legs, gripping my dick, trying to draw him harder. He said, "Oh, lady! That's wild; Joe, with her cunt she's crushing my dick!" And I had a moment of claustrophobic panic as the massive body of Bill weighed heavily upon me. Shock, a sort of surprise, was quickly replaced by some sort of wonder as Bill pushed his hips back, pulling his mighty organ up, up, out and out, slick with my nectar, the massive head rubbing against my vagina walls; then he sat his pulsing dick back into me with a swift push. I screamed out in delight and excitement as he started pumping.

His cock was sliding in and out, in and out, his belly grinding into me, his cock's root mashing my clit with every down stroke, his cock's felt like taking me out every time we pulled out, boom! He pushed me up and down again and again. I could hear his balls start slamming against my anus I responded thrusting him for thrust. I could feel our bodies grinding as he fucked me wetly together. He bent more against me, his head and rugged hair against my shoulder and neck, his thickly matted chest wondrously mashing my boobs as his snake slithered in and out of me, his ball sack flapping over me with each grunting thrust; my pussy jumping up to meet him pressing for the drive.

I could feel my juices slipping down my asshole as he pounded his tool into me; my thighs pistoned back and forth and my palms clenched his butt as we humped and humped, grunting, the bed trembling as we fucked and fucked and fucked.

I could sense the sweat droplets on me. At one point I opened my eyes, which had been firmly closed in pleasure, and saw his ass shaking and clenching again and again over his broad back as He reached forward, thrusting in, out, in and out, his stomach smacking wetly against my tiny frame.

Finally, he pushed himself on his back, then reared on his feet, his heavy rope all that bound up our bodies. "Behold, Joe," he said, breathing heavily. I whimpered in embarrassment and wanted to hump his dick. I was so close to getting cumming.

Smiling, Bill said, "Rub her clit while I catch my breath."

Joe reached over and softly began rubbing my clit with two fingertips, as engorged as she had ever been and sticking out of her hat. He rubbed me in a circle and applied light pressure. Ahhhhhh, I was feeling like he was rubbing up. I stood up on my knees and watched with increasing satisfaction, my palms pinched and my thumbs pinched on my blood-thick nipples.

I could see the red cock of Bill pulsating between us, as Joe squeezed my clit. Every now and then I could see Joe's fingertips brushing Bill's cock, running along with the cunt-juice-covered slippery organ. I could see that the public hair of Bill, like mine, was damp and matted from our fucks. I glanced at Bob, watching Joe approach us both. After a little bit, Joe alternated between rubbing my clit and ring Bill's cock and masturbat him. For me, two or three pumps; then two or three pumps for Joe. It was vicious.

Bill gave an encouraging smile. "Oh, Joey, that feels good. That feels good..." I rolled my pelvis up and down, my pussy hitting Joe's hand as it slid down Bills long, red, wet dick and pressed against my clit sending electrical jolts across my tummy and popping out of my sensitive, bloated, and pleased nipples. This was the best; the best sex I have ever had, by far. This is nothing I have done before, a physical and sensory turn-on and I wished it shouldn't end but for a reason or two, it has to end.

When my climax progressed, I remember my feet and hands getting numb, running up my legs and back, paralysing me. I lost feeling in my neck, and the rictus reached my lips and felt big and puffy. I heard a deep moan rising to a yell as it hit from a distance. I spasmed with the fat head of Bill's dick trapped in me again and again, his shaft being stroked by Joe and my clit pounded over and over again.

It was a continuous organsm. I had some sort of out of body experience. When Bill leaned back over me and started sliding his big dick all the way back into my pussy I felt a little disconnected from moving on. I could sense it filling me up, but it was as though I had anesthetic. He started pumping me in and out again. I felt my hands flailing back and forth as he went in and out of me. My hips began to comply and my body sprung up and fell under him as he fucked me. As he pumped and pumped, my hands squeezed his arms, this massive, fat dick alternately filling me, then vacating, then expanding, the big bulbous head massaging my vagina walls causing such beautiful, beautiful sensations.

Soon the speed of his thrusts accelerated until he grunted a final time or two, plunging his cock deep, deep, deep into me and filling my pussy with its heated sperm as sensation returned to me. It all looked like a river pouring to say the least. With each jet of sperm I could feel his heated cock throb as it splashed inside me and somehow the still moist sensation inside me improves. He stepped over me, in the now super-lubricant, his cock sliding off.

"Goddamn, baby, you're a hot little little one!" he screamed, breathing heavily. Via sleepy eyes I looked at him, then grinned.

"You're one hot cock," I replied feeling saturated.

Abruptly, with one oily tug followed by a slight "ping" sound, he pulled his slimy dick out of my swollen cunt. He went on kneeling with our joint cum between my spread legs, his dick, crimson and shiny, sticking out from the wet nest of red pubic hair. When he moved away, his chest, broad and round, swayed gently, moving the bed when his weight changed.

"Take her down, Joe," he said.

"With enjoyment," answered Joe, stepping about and lying between my spread thighs. He wrapped his arms around my hips, running fingertips across my vaginal folds and exposing me to his eyes. He glanced at my pussy, then at Bill and said, "Look at all this semen, Bill, it's just oozing from her cunt." I saw Bill, nude, his dick falling over his massive balls, all filled with our cum, his hands on his thighs, laughing, smiling. "Lick it up" he ordered.

I sensed Joe's warm breath on my delicate folds and then felt his tongue slipping into my hole. I laid back and enjoyed my sex with the touch of his lips, his tounge sliding in and over my fresh-fucking pussy. My one hand drove down to grab his scalp, and with his tongue he tasted my anus, licking up Bill's and my juices. My other hand was massaging my breasts, and pinching my nipples.

I was very hanging, kind of floating. Yet, then, Joe's lips and tongue found my oh-so-sensitive clit, and he started sucking on it softly. I felt the flames building up again inside of me as he flicked his tongue along my hot button and occassionally twitched his lips and sucked me inside.

I orgasmed again, without warning not as strong as Bill, but a terrific detonation of gratification from my pussy extending the enthralling feelings outward. I squeezed Joe's head between my knees as my body became convulsed, holding him firmly for a spell at my age.

Then I relaxed instantly. Joe got up between my now wide open legs and momentarily fingered my pussy. "Damn, she's soooo slick," he said, mounting me. Without hesitation, his dick slipped deep inside me. I remember his balls hitting me and his cock ground on my pelvis, squeezing my tired clit among us. I laid my palms on his shoulders, and felt the muscles moving as he fucked me. Opening my eyes I looked at him and saw his lips and lip all sparkling in the lamplight, coated in my cum and Bill's semen. He looked happy and soooooo.

Quickly, Joe started pumping me in and out. I kind of laid in a sexual coma like he was raping me. I could hear the soft smacking sounds made by our bodies, as he thrust his cock deep into me. My hips started to rise after a bit and sink in counterpoint to his plunging dick. My hands then grasped his ass-cheeks, and with each out and in motion I could feel them opening and closing. He leaned on mine with his chest, mashing my boobs into my ribcage and pressing his head on my shoulder.

We swayed together in the groove of agelessness before suddenly he came, his sperm ejecting from his cockhead into my moist depths. Just before his hot seed splattered over my cervix I could feel penis stretch. It looked perfect..

There's a lot more to say about that evening, except for Bill saying"... we'd best call it a night." I was pretty sore and feeling a kind of wrung out, so I was grateful for his thoughtfulness.

Joe stayed with me, and we showered in the dingy tub, drying off with the motel's cheap-too-small towels. I had to fold up some of the inexpensive toilet paper and put it in my panties ' ass, as I was still dripping semen when I was dressing. It wasn't even 9 when I had Joe dropping me off by the boardwalk, where I joined some of my buddies who were my own age, wishing the red chaffing on my neck would go down until I went home.

As it turned out, you would never have known the next morning that I had my first three-some, and that the fattest and so far only uncircumcised dick I've ever seen has completely fucked me in. Joe had a hard time looking at me when I returned to work the next morning but with a quick trip to the store room I fixed his nervousness.

Yum. Yum. Muha

The MILF Nurse and The Hot Biker

Annie was just going about her business at the hospital, making her nurse's rounds and caring for her patients. She was 'warned' about one particular new patient, but in her career she had seen it all so she was not worried. The minute she lays eyes on the biker, Stone, her world gets rocked. And then things heat up.

It was another long day at the hospital, moving from one drab room to the next. Most people do not realize how exhausting it can be to take care of sick and injured patients all day long. I stopped about halfway through my shift to eat my very dull frozen meal for lunch before returning to the list of patients that needed attending.

I had been doing this for almost fifteen years now, and that was just this shift… I had taken care of all sorts of people, but this simple recovery wing was one of the easier ones. The only way I found to liven up my work day was to wear my white nurse's dress in a size too tight. I loved the way the male patients would light up at the sight of me and their wives would just scowl in my direction. It was not my fault I was blessed with ample cleavage and a nice firm behind. Granted, it was my fault those features were accentuated by a push-up bra and a G-string. But a working woman has to have her fun somehow. And I always got the best reviews after my sponge baths. Every so often I had a little fun with a lesbian, but that was a rare treat. Most of the time it was just a harmless little boost to my ego and to the patient's. I mean, who hasn't had the naughty nurse fantasy, right? Now I don't wear thigh high stockings and 4-inch heels, but that's just not realistic. I don't wear hose at all!

"Hey, Annie," one of my fellow nurses called out as I headed down the plain gray hallway.

"Oh, hi Charlotte," I replied.

"You catch a look at the new guy in 608?"

"No, not yet. I think he's on the end of my list. I'll swing by."

"Take a good long look," the younger woman grinned.

I furrowed my brow in confusion and moved to the first room on my afternoon list. It was an older man who was recovering from a mild heart attack. The look on his face when I strutted into his room gave me mild concern that he was headed into another heart attack right there. His eyes raked over the swell of my breasts and curve of my hips.

"Mr. Thornton, how are we today?" I grinned brightly.

"Oh much better now. Sponge bath time?"

I chuckled, "Not today. Your chart says that you get to shower today and that you will be doing with a male attendant."

He pouted, "That doesn't sound nearly as fun."

"Mr. Thornton!" I feigned insult and innocence, "What on earth would happen if I got this pretty white dress wet?"

His eyes widened and his hips twitched noticeably.

I laughed, "Seems that your blood flow is working just fine."

I bent over him to check his IV port and made sure to give him an eyeful of cleavage for his efforts. I swayed my hips for him as I left, feeling a little better about the day after his reactions.

The next room was a middle-aged woman who had recently had knee surgery. I was much more business-like and to-the-point with her and she did not seem to have the same appreciation for my outfit as the previous patient.

For the next couple of hours, I moved from room to room as I harmlessly flirted with the male patients and calmly took care of the female ones. I did have a good laugh in one room. I tried so hard to flirt and be cute until finally the sweet man politely informed me that he was gay. I ended up staying a little while longer than necessary just to chat with him. The straight women always tried to rush me out and the straight men always tried to keep me there a little longer. It was nice to just chat with someone about the weather and theatre and things.

Charlotte came bobbing up to me with about an hour left in my shift.

"Annie, did ya see him yet? Did ya?" she inquired anxiously.

I laughed, "Down girl, we get guys in here all the time. And no, I haven't."

"Oh we don't get guys like this one very often…" she winked at me.

"What is so all-fired special about this patient?"

"He broke his leg in a motorcycle accident."

"So?"

"So he needs sponge baths…"

I sighed loudly with irritation. "Charlotte. I don't really care about one patient over the other. I just spent a lovely half hour talking to the man in 617 and it was the best visit of the shift. What is so special about a broken leg from a stupid motorcycle accident?"

Charlotte shook her head, "I'm about to leave but I'll ask you about him again tomorrow. Then we'll see."

I sighed and shook my head at the silly young thing. Sure we got some interesting patients occasionally, but nothing to get worked up over. A local television star maybe or some aging retired musician but none of that had ever really impressed me.

My pulse did speed up at the thought of a bad-ass motorcycle man but it was much less sexy when you thought about him hooked up to monitors and drooling on his pillow. That is how most of my patients look.

I finally reached the end of my list and realized that the only patient I had left to check on was the motorcycle man in question. I stopped at the breakroom for a glass of water and nearly slapped my own cheek for being so nervous.

Stupid Charlotte, I swore at my coworker, has me all nervous about checking on this guy. He can't be all that special. No one is.

I knocked on the door and waited.

"Come in," a deep voice rumbled from the other side.

I took a deep breath and swung the door open. My tummy fluttered at the sight of him and I was in trouble.

****

I was sunk from the moment I laid eyes on his arms as they lay on the white hospital sheets. They were scarily muscular, with tattoos covering almost every inch of skin. His scalp was covered in the prickle of dark hair but judging from the tanned skin, he normally kept it shaved. His eyes were closed but I expected that they would be piercing, right down to the core of my body.

He had one leg sticking out from under the sheets, and it was in a cast up to about mid-thigh. The rest of him almost appears nude from the way the sheets were draped but that would be very strange. He should at least be in a hospital gown.

I moved quietly around the room to check the monitors and the IV port. As I bent over to check the heart beat display, I heard a rustle behind me. I straightened up and whirled around in one fluid motion and found myself staring into the bluest eyes I had ever seen.

And I was right, they looked through my own eyes and down into the depths of me. The golden tan on his face showed signs of hours in the sun but it was smooth and unlined. He was grinning at me and I realized that I had nearly popped clean out of the top of my dress.

"Well hey there," he drawled slowly.

"G-Good evening Mr. Bilstrom."

"Now, now, call me Stone, everyone does."

I nodded, "S-Sure."

His eyes raked over my tight white dress, stopping much longer than necessary at the generous cleavage that was now visible above the top. I kept an extra button unfastened all the time, and having ben bent over, my breasts were thrust up and forward over the top fastened one.

"So, Stone," I tried to collect myself, "how are we doing today?"

He reached one arm up over his head to prop himself up and I watched as his bicep bunched and bulged with each motion.

"Much better now…"

The sheet had slipped down his body and I realized that he was distinctly not wearing his hospital gown.

"Um, Mr. Bilstrom? Where is your gown?"

He dragged his eyes away from my cleavage to look down at his chest, and then back up at me. I could not take my eyes off the flat hard planes of his chest or the hint of cut abs at his waist. One of his pecs had a circle of names tattooed on it and I was curious about it but I could not ask.

"Got tired of wearing a dress," he replied cheekily.

"That's standard issue attire. We can't have you walking around the hospital nude."

He twisted his lips into a wry grin, "Does it look like I'm walking anywhere right now?"

He pointed at the cast on his leg.

I giggled nervously, "Very true."

How had I been reduced to a simpering teenager in his presence? I was going to kill Annie when I saw her the next day. She had totally set me up and she had been totally right about him.

I checked his chart and internally groaned deeply. He was scheduled for a sponge bath that day. I ran my hand over my ponytail and looked at him again.

"So how did you injure your leg?" I asked out of curiosity.

"Ah. Laid down the bike on a ride. I've been recouping

in a different hospital but they moved me over here last night for rehab. Guess I'm in for the long haul, even after this comes off." He patted his large palm against the cast.

"Sounds like it," I nodded.

"Sponge bath day?" he grinned, "I do keep track you know. Every other day it seems."

I nodded, "Today's the day."

He pushed the sheet all the way down to just below his navel. As I stood and stared, I could see the smattering of dark hair spread out on his smooth chest, and the line of curls that trailed from his navel down below the sheet. The thin sheet was draped casually across his groin but I was intensely aware of the outlines underneath it. And it looked shockingly generous even covered.

He appeared to be nearly ten years younger than me, but he was still leering at me as I fumbled with my paperwork.

"I-I-I'll be right back, I need to get my things."

"Hurry back," he grinned and threw his second arm behind his head with the first one.

I closed the door to his room when I left, and found

myself panting in the hallway. A nurse I did not know strolled by and looked at me strangely but I let her think whatever she wanted to think. I was overcome with completely inappropriate lust for my patient.

From the closet, I collected a washcloth, a basin, and some liquid soap for the bath. Normally I didn't mind this portion of my job, but for some reason he made me more nervous than the little old ladies who were nearly overcome with embarrassment. I knew how to handle them. What I did not know how to handle was this horny biker who seemed to be coming on to me. I loaded all the supplies on a cart and headed back to Stone's room.

When I reentered the room, he was still reclining on the bed and had propped it up for a better angle.

"Make sure that water is nice and warm," he cautioned.

"Oh? No cold showers today?" I could not stop the words from spilling out of my lips.

He quirked one eyebrow up at me and waited for me to backpedal on my statement. I stood my ground and stared him down, determined to win back the upper hand in this situation.

He grinned at me, "I'd prefer not, but thank you."

I pushed the cart to the side of his bed and felt his eyes

watching every move my generous curves made. This was going to be one for the memory banks, I could just tell.

****

Stone grinned at me as I started arranging the items for the sponge bath. I lifted the basin to the sink and waited for the water to warm up. The idea of a cold sponge bath made me giggle, but I did not think that would make the patient happy. And besides, I did not necessarily want this sexy guy to cool back down.

Once the water was warm to the touch, I filled the basin and carefully carried it back. I was not careful enough, however, and by the time I reached the side of the bed, I had sloshed just enough on the front of my white dress to make it slightly transparent. My cheeks felt flush when I met his gaze, and he just laid there with those muscular arms propped up behind his head, grinning like a Cheshire cat.

I squirted some of the liquid soap into the basin and dunked the washcloth. As I swirled the water around to lather the soap, I of course managed to slosh just a little bit more on my dress.

"Who's getting the bath here?" he chuckled, pointing at the front of my dress.

I flushed a deeper shade of pink, and tried to think of anything but the way he was leering at my now see-through dress. It was clinging damply to my breasts and pressing up against the lace of my bra. My nipples felt tight and I was certain he could see them.

I finally withdrew the washcloth from the basin and wrung it out slightly. I brushed the warm cloth over his chest and felt the hardness of his muscles under my touch.

"Oh you can do better than that," he smirked, pulling his arms from behind his head.

I dunked the cloth again and started massaging it onto one of his arms more thoroughly. His bicep flexed and I jumped just a little.

"Are you always this nervous? You must be a piece of work around the old men."

"I am not! And they are usually dressed!"

He laughed, "Fair enough. But I'm not the dress wearing type."

Without even thinking it through, I leaned across his body to wash his other arm. My breasts were pressed against his chest and he felt warm underneath me. I finished that arm quickly, and moved to his chest.

"Wh-Wh-What is the circle for?" I asked tentatively as I rubbed the rough cloth over his skin.

"Oh that? It's the names of club members who've died."

"Club members?"

"Yeah, the country club. We like to golf."

I jerked my head up to look at him, and he laughed.

"Biker club babe, biker club."

"Ohhh," I mumbled feeling like a complete idiot.

I slowly moved the cloth down his hard chest to the cut abs of his stomach. He was leaning back on the stack of pillows and closely watching my hands. The sheet stopped just at the top of his pubic bone, and my hands stopped there as well. I moved to the other side of him and started washing the good leg after pulling the sheet back delicately.

My hands moved higher and higher as I bathed him, and I could not help but notice that his legs were slowly moving further apart. And I could not stop my eyes from settling briefly on the outline of something between his thighs. Either the sheet was very flattering or he was one of the most endowed men I had ever seen in person. I stopped just shy of his hip bone, but my eyes lingered at his long muscular leg sticking out from the thin hospital sheet.

I moved to the exposed foot of his broken leg and washed it gently, trying not to disturb the injured limb. I finally finished and rinsed the cloth in the basin.

"What about the rest of me?"

His gaze made my body flush and warm and I fidgeted with the cloth in the basin.

"The rest of you?"

"Oh yes, I need to be thoroughly bathed."

He had now parted his legs as far as they would go.

"We, ah, we don't bathe everything."

He stared at the translucent dress clinging to my full breasts and slowly dragged his eyes to my face.

"I don't think most of them are done as a wet tee shirt contest either."

I gasped and tried to cover myself, but in my infinite wisdom, I chose to cover myself with the soaking wet washcloth.

"Holy hell," he breathed.

The dress was now soaking wet and clinging to every curve, my dark pink nipples very apparent through the thin dress and the lace bra. This time I was certain I saw his cock twitch under the sheet.

"God they're amazing," he muttered as one arm reached out towards me.

Watching this muscular biker reach for my body sent the heat spiraling through my core until it throbbed between my thighs. I could not stop myself from stepping forward into his touch. His thick fingers were surprisingly gentle as they slowly traced the outside curves.

"Come here," he growled, reaching out with the other hand.

When I leaned forward over him, he ran both palms over the front of my dress until they met at the nape of my neck. He pulled me down to him and kissed me hungrily. His teeth nipped at my lower lip and his tongue demanded entrance. I heard myself moan as I granted him access and felt his plunder my mouth.

One hand kept my mouth against his while the other slid down my back and dug in to my ass firmly. He devoured my mouth as my tits pressed up against his bare chest. I could feel the heat from his body seeping into mine, and it was all spiraling down to my pussy.

My hands were still clenched at my side and I finally gave in. I ran my fingertips over his chest and felt him quiver. I locked my fingers behind his neck and pulled him to me.

He groaned and slid his mouth down my jawline to my neck. Stone nibbled the pulse that pounded in my neck and I moaned softly against his ear.

I suddenly heard shuffling outside the door and I snapped back away from him. I scurried to lock the door and took a deep breath before turning around to face him. He beckoned to me with one finger and a devilish grin.

I had collected just enough of my wits to see clearly that this gorgeous hunk of a biker wanted me. And he was trapped in that bed for me to enjoy.

I tossed my ponytail and grinned as I slowly walked back to him. With each step, I unfastened another button on the dress. He leaned back and watched the slow striptease while one hand lightly squeezed his growing cock.

When I reached the side of his bed, I was wearing nothing but the lace bra and matching G-string. I popped the sides of his bed down and crawled on top to straddle his hips. I ground lightly against the thickness between his thighs and he groaned deeply.

"Oh jeezus," he muttered.

"Has it been long?" I winked innocently.

"You don't want to know."

I laughed and slipped one hand between our bodies to feel his thickness.

As I tormented him through the sheet, I asked again, "Tell me…"

"Almost two weeks, since my accident."

"Not even one chance to touch yourself?"

"No, the damn nurses wouldn't leave me alone!"

I laughed, "And here I am! Should I leave you to your own devices?"

"Oh god, no, please… you have to…"

"I have to what?"

"Help me out…"

I sat up just enough to pull the sheet down further and his cock sat long and thick against his thigh. His sack looked full and heavy and swollen. I ran my fingernails over the length of his shaft and tickled his balls.

"Oh fuck," his lips twisted at the tormenting touch.

I tickled and teased every inch of him, never lingering too long in one spot. As I slowly and loosely stroked him, his nails raked up my back, making me arch towards him. He flicked the clasp of my bra loose and my full firm breasts popped loose. He grabbed the nape of my neck roughly and pulled me forward to clasp one stiff nipple in his lips. As he licked and sucked, I could feel it grow tighter in his mouth. He teased them back and forth until I lost my focus on his cock and let it slip from my hand.

"Oh god, don't stop," he pleaded.

I kissed his hard, letting my stiff nipples rake against his chest as I slid down his body. Nestled between his thighs, I could see just how hard he was. It was bobbing in the air, begging for attention.

I held his cock against his lower stomach and ran my tongue from the base to the tip. His groans spurred me on and I licked again and again.

"Oh fuck," he moaned, gripping the mattress.

I licked every inch until he was slippery and hard in my fist, and I stroked him while my mouth latched to the head. I flicked my tongue over the sensitive spot just under the ridge and sucked firmly. My other hand kept kneading and tickling his heavy balls until his hips started to buck.

"Oh god, oh fuck," he groaned.

I felt his sack tighten up towards his body and the head of his cock swelled and pulsed. I sunk my mouth as far down as I could and stroked him faster until I felt the first jet hit my tongue. I milked and stroked every last drop down my throat until he flopped backwards onto the bed, panting for air.

"C'mere," he reached for my bare shoulder.

I inched back up his body, letting him feel my silky skin slide against his. When I ran my tongue over his salty neck, he started reaching and grabbing and twisting at my body. I finally gave in to whatever he was trying, and found myself straddling his face and looking at his feet.

"Take it off," he growled at me.

I wriggled my hips until the G-string slid free and I tossed it to the corner of the room. His hands grabbed my hips roughly and pulled me against his face. When his lips pressed against my wetness, I writhed against him, eager for pleasure of my own.

His tongue slipped easily between my folds and I groaned when he found my throbbing little nub. He teased my ache, sliding from my clit to my opening and back again. Never staying in one place long enough to help the urgent throbbing he had started.

"Oh god," I moaned softly, urgently rubbing against his face to find what I needed.

His hands reached up and one of them grasped my ass cheek roughly while the other pinched and rolled my nipples. They seemed directly connected to my aching clit and I arched my back for more. He finally caught my clit between his teeth and flicked the tip of his tongue over the taut swollen surface until I bucked and dug my nails into his heaving chest. This time he didn't let up, and as he flicked he slid two fingers deep inside my slippery wetness.

"Fuck me," I begged as I squirmed my hips against the onslaught of sensations.

He rubbed his tongue harder and pounded his fingers inside me, urging me on, shoving me closer and closer to climax. I could hardly breathe as I scaled the peak. He finally stuffed three fingers into my tight warm wetness and curled them just right against that textured little place inside.

"There, there, there," I chanted, praying he would keep doing it.

And within moments, the stars swirling behind my eyes exploded into light and I soaked the poor guy's face and hand and chest with my climax. I could feel my body clenching and clutching at his fingers as my clit contracted under his tongue.

"Oh god, oh Stone," I cried out, clutching at his hips as I writhed.

When I fell back from the peak, I twisted and slipped in the bed until I was curled up next to his good side. Our hearts pounded as we caught our breath and he leisurely wrapped one muscled arm around my waist.

****

So admittedly, that was easily one of the hottest sexual experiences of my life. I say "one of" not to diminish it in any way, but to highlight that the first time is always a little more special than the others. The other experience that tops the list was when Stone got out of the hospital and his leg was completely mended...

Oh? Did I not mention that his special sponge baths became a regular thing? Charlotte was so mad when I was assigned to be his only nurse but I sure didn't mind.

The day after that first one, she came bounding up to

me bubbling over about him. Through a pure miracle, I managed to keep the smirk off my face as I told her he was no big deal. She scoffed at me and stormed off in a huff but I did not really care at that point.

I was not there the day Stone got released but he called me before he had even left the parking lot. His buddies had driven up there to meet him, and he told them to drop him at my apartment before making any other stops.

He walked in, with only a slight limp, and proceeded to drag me off to the bedroom. I had touched and tasted his cock so many times, I was literally dripping to feel him inside me and that sweet tattooed muscular man did not disappoint. He filled and stretched me in so many ways, I still get tingles thinking about it.

By the time he slid inside me that first evening, it had been nearly a month since he had had sex and the grin on his face lit up my world. He took me three times that night, and twice more in the morning. We fucked in the bed, on the couch, in the kitchen, and in the shower.

It has been a few months now, and we are still seeing each other. I was a little nervous to get involved with someone who was a confirmed member of a biker gang, but everyone has turned out to be super great. They love to hear the story about the first time Stone and I met, and I can always see a few twitching cocks when we tell it.

Sometimes one of the cheekier members will ask if I still have the nurse's outfit and I just smile primly. But I think the grin on Stone's face gives it away every time.

A Straightforward MFM Threesom

As his last sensual adventure left off, Derek presently had two different yet completely exhilarating experiences with couples. The first couple was really a straightforward MFM threesome encounter where both the husband and he played with the wife and the second couple was a cuckolding adventure where Derek fucked the wife's brains out in the absence of the husband.

Derek immediately discovered that once couples started investigating his profile on various swinging sites, his success rate surged up from 1 to 100 in a split second. Discovering decent, respectful, discreet and attractive single men is always a daunting task for couples and once the trust and confidence are proven it is like the floodgates are opened for sensual adventures. Derek began turning down many couples than ones he decided to talk to.

Being a matured, suave and hung fellow in his late thirties, and surely with his exotic voice and polite manners, he was always successful to make an impression on couples, especially the wives. Besides, his hazel eyes were too intoxicating to be denied the savage temptation of mind-blowing sex. Someone has correctly said, "Great sex starts with the eyes, follows the mind and explores the body." And Derek lived to prove the proverb.

In due course of time, Derek found himself talking with a decent couple, Laura and Bruce over a swinging dating app, who were also searching for a decent person to fulfill their twisted fantasies. Bruce was 44 and Laura was 36, so she was truly near his age by then. At first, they simply wanted to discuss about the lifestyle as they were novice and amateur to the concept and idea. They were thinking they needed a person to become acquainted with, and inevitably hang out and possibly she would give a hand-job or a blowjob to get things started comfortably.

Typically, Derek never played with novice couples and he had already made up his mind to deny any further proceedings. But this time, a thunderbolt struck him when he saw the real picture of Laura in his message box; Laura was truly ravishing and incredibly attractive. She was a natural blonde, 5'5", pleasant D boobs and had a stunning curvy body, something which always grabbed Derek's attention. She had an Austrian look to her with smooth facial lines and a captivating smile. To finish it off she was an Aerobics coach at a nearby gym and had the body to appear with rippled abs and waist, strong legs, and a buxom booty ass. Derek was desperate to see it naked and bare right from that moment when he saw her photograph.

They chatted online for some time before deciding to meet at a bar for drinks one night. It was a classy bar with lots of people gathering to chill out on a Friday night. They grabbed their drinks and settled down on an empty high -top table where they could chat comfortably. It was normal small talk, life, sports, climate, holidays, likings with a few laughs. It never got too flirty or truly went down to something sexual during their discussions, despite a couple of endeavors by Derek to push it that way.

They all returned home after their Friday rendezvous and that was apparently that. Soon thereafter at around 3 am (Derek saw it the next day) the couple had texted him enquiring as to whether he was available and could meet again the following night. So Derek gave it another shot and showed up. The earlier night Laura had been wearing a skintight backless red dress exhibiting her provocative cleavage. An incredible change.

Derek could tell immediately that the tone and transformation were extraordinary and Laura appeared to be more friendly and relaxed. The discussion soon drifted into more sexual and kinky topics after a few drinks and they continued to devour a significant number of glasses than the earlier night. At a certain point, Laura even bowed down before Bruce and Derek, unnecessarily grabbing a dropped napkin. It was a fabulous view of her buxom booty ass in the tight red dress. Derek, even for a moment thought that Laura purposely exhibited her panties to their secret appreciation and temptation.

After a few more drinks and a little more talking and giggling, Derek finally decided to break the ice, "Anybody keen on heading to my place to have a couple of more drinks, probably something else? Possibly we might chill out in a much more relaxed environment."

Bruce reacted animatedly, "That sounds great! How far do you live from here?"

"Oh, don't worry! It's just a ten minutes' walk. Let's go then. Just follow my car." Derek seemed excited too.

"Great! We should do it. But we'll have to ride your car since we got here by an Uber cab," Laura finally consented.

When Bruce and Laura got in Derek's car, Laura had suddenly gone somewhat quieter than before, maybe nervous at the thrilling opportunities knocking her sensual door. They hopped in the car, Laura was in the center. As they drove, they kept on chatting and Derek made the first move and kept his hand on her thigh close to her knee at a certain point. Derek could practically sense Laura shivering in anticipation. He left it there as they proceeded with the short drive and arrived at Derek's residence.

They moved out and headed inside where Derek fixed a few beer cans and they almost settled in their places, Laura and Bruce on the couch and Derek on a big seat to her opposite side. Sooner or later, she adjusted her legs, flashing a glimpse of her red panties which Derek realized must be too small as he had not seen anything when she had bowed down before in the bar to grab the napkin from the floor.

Rapidly the discussion turned sexual and Derek asked Laura, "What's your opinion about holding another man's cock?"

She chuckled and reacted, "Well, it certainly is a new idea, threatening idea, yet it turns me on."

"So, you've never played with another cock?" Derek teased.

"Well, not after my marriage, saw a couple earlier." Laura chuckled.

By then Derek chose to be bold and to join them on the sofa, Laura was now sandwiched between them.

"Possibly tonight is the night to spread your wings and

give it a shot." Derek teased again.

Laura turned toward Bruce and said, "Yes, I too think tonight is the perfect night."

Bruce had begun to gently caress her thigh, getting closer and closer to the end of her sexy dress. Derek joined in enthusiastically, massaging the other thigh as she kept her hand over Derek's and somewhat spread her legs in excitement. Bruce unzipped his jeans and his hard throbbing cock was obvious under his briefs. Laura reached over and liberated his hardened cock out from the briefs opening; his cock shook hard in sensual anticipation. He was on the little side regardless of being fit and tall, most likely just 5" with an average thickness.

Laura grabbed the base and began stroking the erection, making simple movements measuring his whole shaft. Derek accepted the opportunity to move his hand up her thigh and slip it under the dress. He gradually moved his way to her pussy (which was not a long way from the end of her sexy dress) and gently caressed the outside of her thong. It was already wet and he could undoubtedly feel her pussy lips as he pushed the thong together. Laura groaned a little and laid back as she was all the while stroking Bruce's cock.

Two or three minutes passed by like this, Derek massaging around Laura's thong and pussy, moving the thong around to tease her various sensitive parts in between her legs. At that point, Bruce suddenly blew his load of cum, one decent shot a foot in the air and afterward a little dribble on his wife's hand.

She turned toward Derek and said, "Your turn" and immediately began unzipping his jeans. Within a minute, she had pulled his foot-long hard cock out of his briefs and praised his enormous cock before getting the base and giving a long stroke. She clearly appreciated stroking cock and was an expert at it; Derek realized why Bruce couldn't keep going on for long. Laura was gliding her hand up and down, getting his whole shaft from the base and up to the head. "Wow! You're such an expert," Derek winked at Laura.

Bruce was observing his wife's erotic ministrations, obviously pleased and getting hard once more. Derek's hand was still on Laura's pussy, and he decided to quit teasing her and moved the now soaked thong aside and slid two fingers in. Her pussy resembled the rest of her body, not small but rather totally strong and tight sucking in his fingers. Derek began finger fucking her as she increased the pace of her expert hand job and they both began groaning, getting intensely aroused by the mutual satisfaction.

Bruce reached over and got her other hand and returned it on his flaccid cock. She began stroking his cock which came to life within moments of Laura's initiation of lively and exciting Hand jobs. She was stroking both her men simultaneously, without missing a beat. Bruce reclined on the sofa as she did this and closed his eyes. Derek accepted this opportunity to utilize his other hand to guide her head down his huge cock. She didn't hesitate at all and immediately gobbled up his giant fuck-pole, working her way to deep throat. It took Bruce a couple of moments to acknowledge what she was doing; however, Laura continued deep-throating Derek and playing with her husband's pin-dick simultaneously.

He blew his load again while watching Laura suck Derek's cock, with him not far behind. Derek shot an enormous load of cum into her mouth while Laura sucking it hard and fast and gulping it like a slut and a hot wife. They all relaxed there on the sofa, Bruce and Derek completely exhausted. Derek afterward proceeded with his fingers slamming her cunt while she spread her legs inviting the eroticism which she inevitably lost letting cum hard on his fingers.

From that point it didn't take Derek long to feel the desire and get hard once more, his glistening long cock gradually hardening and picking up shape as a big fat cock. Laura stood up and said she was going to change but before she could leave Derek stepped up to and spanked her ass a couple of times that was secured firmly by her short sexy dress. She turned around and grinned at him and Derek grabbed her waist and pulled her down onto his lap.

Now, she was sitting with her back to him, straddled over his lap with her thong covered ass on his groin. Derek's hard cock was shooting up before her pussy, facing her soaked red panties covering her pussy. He stretched around and slid a hand down her thong caressing her drenched clit and making her groan. He kept at it for a couple of moments until she was groaning hard before Derek immediately pulled her up a little high and planted her over his giant fuck-pole. Her small soaked panties were perfectly drifted away from the path as she removed it by herself, clearly, she was burning with savage wants. Thus, her panties exhibited no hindrance and Derek's potent manhood slid directly into her tight yeaning pussy.

Laura let out a boisterous gasp as Derek's monster cock stuck around 2/3rds of the way, and she tried to lift herself off it. She saw her husband Bruce as if to apologize but instead was surprised to discover him effectively stroking his flaccid cock. He gently assured her, "It's okay hon, go for it, live your night" and continued stroking his cock watching his wife's adulterous adventure and getting intensely turned on by it.

Laura gently eased herself back down; gradually taking Derek's entire length until her juicy married cunt had taken its balls deep. He could feel her pussy wrapped firmly around his throbbing cock, apparently, her pussy muscles were squeezing his cock. It was an incredible sensation. She started to bounce up and down, gradually in the beginning and afterward harder until she was bouncing from the tip of his bulbous cock head right down to his balls at a quick pace. She was going so quick and taking the whole length that Derek was stressed that she would go excessively far and miss in transit down. Be that as it may, she didn't, she rode him perfectly burning with savage wants and quenching her buried lusts.

Derek let Laura bounce that ass for a couple of moments while striving hard not to blow his load inside her as her amazing legs and ass rode his cock. Derek at that point delicately grabbed her waist and hindered her fast rhythm, letting her feel every inch of his fuck-pole entering and leaving her. As he felt himself getting closer to an overwhelming orgasm, Derek stood up, with her still appended to his cock, spun her around so she was face down on the sofa and began fucking her hard in the doggy style. He, in the end slid her to the floor and had her go face down to the carpet on the floor with her ass up in the air. Finally, he was standing up behind her and jack hammering practically straight down into her married juicy pussy.

Laura was groaning hard and loud and Derek was enjoying a slut wife's plight never holding back for a second. Bruce was all the while jacking off and he was groaning likewise and had begun encouraging Derek, instructing him, pleading him to "fuck her", "pound her hard", and so on. Derek started to slap Laura's buxom ass as his cock was extending her pussy beyond limits and destroying it stroke by stroke. He in the long run lost it and exploded somewhere inside Laura and had cum for what is felt like an unending length of time. He blew many loads into her until he was totally depleted, slid his cock out and collapsed on the floor panting hard. Laura too collapsed beside him, gasping and exhausted, and still had the red dress on but utterly manhandled and disheveled. It had cum on it in different areas.

Also, obviously within the sensational fucking adventure, Bruce had cum too and was equally exhausted.

Following a few moments, Bruce shouted out, "Goodness, that was so hot."

Derek answered, "Surely it was. I loved every moment of it... You're one lucky bastard to marry such a hot girl"

Laura reacted with a smile, "I certainly appreciated it too. I can't believe we waited this long to experience such sensational ecstasy. Looks like I may need to discover a new girl for you to repay the favor."

Bruce shot back, "No sweetie, that was so perfect, you're so perfect. No need to favor me for anything with anything, simply promise you will do it once more."

Laura and Derek grinned at one another, realizing this absolutely wouldn't be the last time.

Not only was it not the last time, yet it likewise wouldn't be the last time that night. Derek and Laura ended up fucking three times more, every time Laura experiencing mind-melting orgasms flying the zeniths of the highest heavens. Even when Bruce decided to take the night's leave in Derek's guest room, there was no stopping or holding back for Laura and Derek, they just couldn't feel and have enough of each other and every time their thirst just grew bigger. Before the night was over, Laura had three loads of cum in her pussy, one on her gorgeous face, one in her mouth and one all over her juicy tits and sexy body. She had ridden Derek in every angle, gotten fucked in the patio hot tub, and gotten jack hammered on countless occasions. Furthermore, the best part was that she laid down with Derek in his bed while Bruce slept in the guest room, Laura's hand always feeling the heat of Derek's potent manhood.

With the first light of the day Derek gave her one final treat, which was feeding her ass with his monster cock while Bruce made the coffee and arranged for the snacks. It took him around ten minutes to perfectly lubricate Laura's ass with enough lube, fingering her and working his cock in her bubble ass to make it work. But in the end, Derek fit cozily inside her incredibly tight ass. Derek put her in doggy style on the lounge chair so she could watch Bruce make coffee as he had his way with her and in the end, loaded her butt-hole up with his cum. Obviously, Bruce was hard the whole time and Laura gave him a quick blowjob a couple of times in between before Derek had ejaculated in her butt-hole.

Bruce and Laura had breakfast and hit the streets, with an incredible memory. They exchanged numbers to keep in touch and wanting to enjoy sensational fucking adventures soon ...

The BBW

Once again, home on a Saturday night alone, all my friends busy with their husbands or wives. Since being divorced I have stayed home a lot except for going to work I pretty much spend a lot of time alone. It's not that I can't attract a man, it just seems I have come to a time in my life where I would just rather not be totally committed to one person. I have not been able to find a man that would be willing to try new things sexually, and also be very dominant and willing to share. Maybe if I could find a man like that, then I would consider getting married again, but of course it's an almost impossible kind of man to find. So here I sit alone, and my pussy wet, and throbbing to be used and raped and I will most likely resort to just masturbating myself to orgasm, fantasizing about one of my many hot, nasty scenarios......Or so I thought.

I decided, after smoking a bit of weed from my little metal pipe, that I would take a ride down to the adult sex store I knew of about fifteen minutes from me. I have been to the store, but never alone and was very nervous, but being stoned helped me get over that. I decided to take the bus since I had smoked, and that was fine with me since the bus stop was right in front of the sex shop. I decided to dress down a bit because I wasn't really looking to do anything extreme, just see the reaction of some horny perverts when I walk in alone. I settled on a tight pair of jeans, and a somewhat tight button down blouse that showed a bit of cleavage. Let me describe myself to you so you can get a better idea of what you would see if you were standing in front of me. I am five feet, two inches tall, two hundred and thirty pounds (BBW), long brown hair, brown eyes, and forty-D chest. Because I am well proportioned no one ever believes that I am as heavy as I am, and have even been told I don't belong in the BBW category, and just say I'm thick. Either way, I am very sexually submissive, and enjoy being degraded, and treated like a slut. You would never know it by my Brooklyn attitude, but I truly love rough nasty sex, and I would love to be owned by one, but used by many.

I stepped onto the bus and found a seat way in the back where it was relatively empty. All except for two older men, about sixty or so, looking me up and down as I approached. I took the seat across from them, and they both turned and smiled as I sat down. They both nodded their heads and said "Good evening," and, I couldn't help but notice that their eyes were fixed on my breasts, which were kind of popping out of my shirt, and with the top three buttons open they got a great view of some cleavage. They were practically drooling, and I have to be honest, it was turning me on so much my pussy was twitching from the attention. They were both overweight, and not much to look at but still turned me on none the less.

"Where are you off to pretty lady?", one of them asked.

"I will be getting off at twenty fifth street", I answered.

"Isn't that an awfully dark part of town?", the other one asked.

"Yes, I guess it is, but that's where the store I'm going to is, so I won't be on the street", I answered.

Our conversation continued, and I found out their names were John, and David, they were both sixty five years old, and single. They joked around about the only store in that area is the sex shop, and with no denial from me a big smile came across my face and I think I even blushed. They both laughed, and asked if I would like some company. I explained to them I have never gone alone, and would much rather this time, but maybe some other time, if we got together. They accepted my answer, and they both slipped me their phone numbers so we could get together 'real soon' as they put it. I put the numbers in my pocket and rang the bell since the next stop was mine. We said out good-byes as the bus slowed to a stop and I stepped off the bus, and watched it pull away as I was left standing there.

I took a deep breathe as I walked towards the front door of the sex shop, and I pulled open the door and stepped inside. It was a lot bigger than I had imagined, and filled with toys, and DVD's. I slowly walked through examining all the toys hanging on the walls, and some inside glass cases. Continuing past the toys, are the DVD's which quite honestly I have never ventured this far into this store before. Any time I cam in here with a fuck buddy, or lover, it had always been to just buy toys, and never actually past that part of the store. I continued to the DVD section and went right to the rape/forced section, and saw so many movies that I know would turn me on. As I scanned the rack of movies, a title did catch my eye, "Degrade This BBW" was the title. I picked up the box, and the picture on the front showed a BBW woman, about forty on her knees sucking a guy's big hard cock. I turned the box over to get a synopsis on the movie, and I what I read was making my pussy wet. The box read: "Watch this fat whore get degraded and used by one man, and sometimes more. Call this whore any nasty name you can think of and she comes back for more." That's, all I had to read and I was already wishing I was the girl in the movie. Why can't I find men like in this movie that enjoy a BBW whore like myself. I began to think that maybe those kind of men were only in the movies.

I didn't notice the two old men from the bus walk in the door since I was so engrossed in reading this box. I heard footsteps coming toward the back section of the store, and I panicked and put the movie back quickly. I would pick it up on my way I thought to myself. As I walked over to another section hidden from the one I was in, David walked up to the rack to see what movie I was looking at. He saw the box, and a big grin surfaced on his old overweight face. He called his friend John over to read the box I had just put down, and they both agreed they would give me what I need.

They sneakily followed me around the store, and then watched me go up the small set of stairs to the movie booths in the very back of the store. I went into one of the rooms, and there was a small screen, and you had to drop a dollar in the machine and a movie would play for five minutes, and a small cushioned bench like chair. . I figured I came here to explore, so explore I will. I locked the door behind me and sat down, and fished in my bag for some singles. I popped the first one in and a menu came up on the screen asking what type of movie I would like to watch. In the search bar I typed "BBW degraded", and hit enter. List popped up with about ten movies, and I chose, "BBW Fuck Meat", and sat back and waited for the movie to begin. It started out with a BBW, about a hundred pound heavier than me, being grabbed by the throat and smacked in the face by a fat older guy, who looked to be about sixty years old. Another one of my fantasies is to be used like a filthy slut by two older, more unattractive perverted men, but that's another story. As I watched and listened to the man degrade her, I could feel my pussy beginning to get very moist.

"You're nothing but a worthless piece of fuck meat, you fat cunt!", he yelled at her.

"No, no please I am not a whore," she pleaded.

"Oh yes you are a whore, and tonight you're my fucking whore!", he whispered in her ear as he clenched his hand around her throat.

The more she pleaded no, the more turned on the old man got, and the more wet my pussy was getting, and I began rubbing my breasts through my shirt. I was imagining this old man using me like that, and my nipples hardened at my tough. I rubbed my breasts as I watched the old man smack the woman in her face, and then he began smacking her breasts, and now my pussy was dripping. I love when a man smacks my breasts, and degrades me while he's doing it. I was so turned on, I actually unbuttoned my jeans and slid them, and my panties down around my ankles. I knew I had locked the door so I assumed I would not get caught if I played a little.

The woman was still screaming no, but wasn't resisting as much as the old man rammed his old fingers up her fat wet pussy. You could see she was beginning to enjoy it as I rubbed my clit and breasts, and imagined I was her. As I continued to watch the camera panned out on the scene and there was another fat old guy sitting on a sofa in the room. He was stroking his cock through his pants as the other man got the whore ready to be the entertainment for the evening. He fingered her pussy, or cunt as he liked to call it, while he called her filthy names. This obviously turned her on because you could hear her moaning now from the use she was getting.

I sat back, closed my eyes and imagined the two men that I saw on the bus earlier were using me right then and there. I imagined them forcing me to my knees to take turns sucking their cocks, while they degraded me and smacked me around. Little did I know they were behind me, letting me get myself hot enough that I would eagerly be a whore for them both.

Just when I was about to come, John cleared his throat behind me, and I jumped up and turned around, and saw John and David from the bus watching me as I pulled up my jeans. They both had a sinister look in their eyes as they took my place on the bench, and unzipped their pants to reveal their hard cocks. John's cock was about seven inches, and David's was about six inches, and both so old and wrinkled looking. I know I should have been trying to find a way to get out of my current situation, but all I could think about was having their cock in all my holes. John woke me out my daze when he ordered me to get to my knees and suck their cocks. My mind said run, but instead I got down on my knees and crawled over to them and took a cock into each hand. I began stroking them as they looked at me like I was nothing more than holes to stick their cocks in, which of course only turned me on more.

"I can stroke my cock myself, get our cocks in that mouth you fat pig whore!", David demanded.

I quickly took David's cock in my mouth, and he grabbed a hand full of my hair and forced me down further onto his cock.

"That's it you fucking fat pig slut, suck that old cock!" David taunted as he force fucked her mouth.

"Get over here and suck my cock too piggy!', John demanded.

I switched over to John's cock, and he followed suit with David and grabbed my hair and forced me down on his old hard cock. I went back and forth for what seemed like forever, and they abruptly stopped and pushed me away.

"Get dressed pig, and come with us," David ordered.

So consumed with lust, and the need for more use I obeyed his orders. I followed them out of the booth, now wondering how they got in, when I saw a sign that read: "Rooms do not lock, if light above door is red please do not enter." I didn't notice that sign before, and was now glad I hadn't. As I followed behind the old men, I heard them discuss that we were going back to John's apartment to do me real good, and when John grabbed the movie I was looking at earlier off the shelf to purchase it, I almost came right there. I was so hot and turned on by now I was really looking forward to some more degrading use by them.

As we stood outside waiting for the bus, they both fondled my breasts and pinched my nipples, making them hard and so visible that the bus driver couldn't stop staring at my breasts as we got on the bus. The bus was completely empty, and they guided me to the back of the bus, and put me in the last corner seat. David sat down next to me, and John stood in front of me and unzipped his pants and pulled out his still hard cock and whispered, "Suck my cock whore." Of course I did as I was told. My pussy was flowing at this point, and when David began pinching my nipples and whispering in my ear what a fat pig I was, I began moaning and they knew they could do whatever they wanted to me, and I wouldn't say no, but I would soon learn they liked to hear a woman say no while they used her anyway. Another nig turn on for me, and I was anticipating what would happen next. We were coming up to our stop, and John rang the bell as he put his hard cock back into his pants. As we walked off the bus the bus driver couldn't help but smile knowing what I was doing back there, and it turned me on to feel like such a whore.

We cam up to a building, and John opened the outside door with his key, and we followed him in. As I walked up the stairs I could feel David's eyes on my ass., so I stuck my ass out a little so he could get a better view. We cam to John's apartment door, and the minute we were in his apartment they grabbed me by my hair and dragged me into the bedroom, and threw me on the bed, as I begged for them to stop, not meaning it of course. I watched as these two old men came at me with nothing more than using me holes on their mind. They quickly pulled my clothes off, and I laid there on my back with John on one side of me and David on the other. Their hands were all over me, and David sucked on my tit, as John fingered my dripping wet cunt.

"Oh yeah!, this fat pig is so fucking wet!", John exclaimed.

John fingered me hard and fast as David abused my tit and told me what a dirty piggy I was.

"Please don't do this, please stop!", I screamed.

That only fueled them more, and now I had both their fingers deep inside my cunt, making me moan and play with my own tit. They each got up to get undressed, as I laid there and played with my pussy for them while I watched them take their clothes off. I watched as they revealed old looking overweight bodies, wrinkled skin, pot bellies, and cocks, which of course I what I needed.

I watched these old bodies climb back onto the bed, and each kneeled down at either side of my head, and forced me to take turns sucking their cocks as they went back to fingering my hot wet cunt. I was bucking wildly on the bed, and when I felt someone's old fingers enter my ass I grabbed both cocks and shoved them into my mouth at once.

"Look at you, you're just a worthless fat pig whore that needs to be used and abused, aren't you?" John asked.

I answered them by the fact I was moaning like a bitch in heat, and I was fucking their old fingers buried inside my holes.

"Oink for us fat piggy!", David ordered.

I took their cocks out of my mouth, and said "Oink oink", and returned to the job at hand. That's when they began smacking my tits, and degrading me more. I was loving every minute of it, and was so happy when David climbed up between my legs, and began sucking on my soaking wet cunt. He licked up and down my slit, and sucked on my clit as he fingered me, making me suck John's cock even harder.

"The piggy loves to have her cunt sucked while she sucks cock, doesn't she?", John asked but knew he wouldn't get an answer since I was to enthralled with the cock in my mouth. They used me like for about twenty minutes, and David got up and John took his place between my legs, and sucked on my cunt for another twenty minutes. By this point I was practically begging to be fucked hard and rough by their old wrinkled cocks. John got up and aimed his cock right for my wet whore cunt, and rammed his cock in me making me scream.

"That's it piggy, take my cock deep inside you fat hole, that's what you are good for!', John taunted. I sucked David's cock hard and fast as John pounded into me. I was in ecstasy, and they switched positions, and David's cock was sliding in and out of my cunt, and I was cleaning my juices off John's cock.

"That's it piggy, get my cock nice and wet so I can rape

that fat ass of yours," John said.

I tried to protest but he just shoved his cock in deeper, making me gag and choke. At the same time John pulled his cock from my mouth, and David slipped his cock out of my cunt, and they roughly turned me over until I was on all fours like a dog for them. David slid under me, and John pushed me onto his old wrinkly cock, and as I rode David John grabbed me by my hair and forced his cock into my mouth, as David smacked my tits, and pinched my nipples. I felt like such a whore bouncing up and down on this old man's cock, while another old cock is filling my mouth. This is what I have always fantasized about, and now it's reality, and I was loving it.

John suddenly pulled his cock from my mouth, and came up behind me and pushed me down on to David smashing my tits against his chest. I then felt John's cock at the opening to my ass, and when I began to protest David smacked me in the face, and John smacked me hard on my ass.

"You're nothing more than a piece of fuck meat for a

cock sandwich, and we will show you!!", John screamed.

John rammed his cock in to my ass hard, making me scream, and he just kept pounding away. After the initial pain of his violation subsided, I actually began to enjoy it. I felt so full and wonderful with these cocks inside me, and I began fucking them back as they filled me.

"Oh yes, yes!, fuck my fat whore holes, yes!", I begged.

That was all they needed to hear, and in a matter of seconds they were filling my holes with their old cum. It seemed like forever before they were empty and got up off their new cum dump. When I thought they were done with me I got up to get dressed, and John stopped me, "What are you doing you fat pig?"

"I'm getting dressed to go," I answered.

"Oh no you're not, we aren't finished with you yet." John

said.

"That's right whore, we took the little blue pill, and we still haven't watched the movie you were so interested in at the sex shop," David chimed in.

"Now get into the bathroom and get cleaned up, so we can continue your use as a piggy whore!" John demanded.

As a fat pig whore does, I got up and went into the bathroom, and imagined what was next for me as their personal fat pig cum dump.

A BDSM Munch

Julia had also started to keep herself upbeat with BDSM knowledge by attending munches. The more she interacted with professional dominatrices, the greater was her knowledge and resolute to express her dominance to Robin. And gradually, their bedroom dominance also shifted to a 24/7 domme/sub relationship. Julia was intrigued to attend a private BDSM munch with Robin. Although he was reluctant in the beginning, she was quite persuasive in her measures. The key thing about this BDSM munch was those elite members of the society, including lawyers, models, businessmen and intellectuals used to attend this very secretive and extremely private BDSM munch. There was a competition among the attendees along with their submissives. The winner would not only benefit monetarily, but also get a chance to attend other BDSM munches all across the globe that were sponsored and organized by them. Also, included was the lucrative deal to share their experiences with other BDSM enthusiasts.

"My slave, I need you to do this."

Robin trembled as Julia peered into his eyes. She was holding his face with her two hands so he was compelled to look back at her.

"We've worked hard for this moment. This is our moment."

There was urgency in her voice. Robin nodded his head and looked down. With that consent, Julia proceeded with her arrangements.

Robin was naked except for his steel chastity confinement. Julia utilized a thick, all-around leather strap to tie his muscular arms to his sides and metal clasps to attach his wrist cuffs to collars at his upper thighs. A subsequent strap pulled his arms back. The stance was significant; she utilized her crop to tenderly remind him to stand upright.

"Alright, now the leash," Julia delicately said as she clipped her leather leash to the ring that was welded onto the ball ring of his chastity cage.

The last item was the blindfold. It was soft leather and accommodated his face, superbly, blocking out all light and vision. Robin always felt better when the blindfold went on, as he was now in his very own private world. When he could see he believed he had some obligation regarding himself, even when bound and vulnerable. Blindfolded and bound, he gave up totally to Julia. He cherished the vibe of being totally in her control!

Julia amazed Robin with a delicate kiss on his lips. Her long light hair brushed against his face. She reassured him that they were prepared and steady and that she was certain he would do great.

A light went ahead implying that the time had come. She gave Robin's chain a delicate pull and he started walking, following her out the door into the little podium. Five hundred women began cheering. Robin couldn't see them, however there were four other men being driven into the center ring. This was the last event of obedience school for men. Every one of the participants had worked hard, trying to perfect their technique and ability to entertain. Julia and Robin were the best, but there could be just one winner.

Julia and Robin were to go third, so she fastened Robin's leash to the post that was there for that reason. The guidelines stated that he was to wait alone, so Julia gave him a friendly squeeze on his left side butt cheek and left. Now Robin felt alone and somewhat frightened. It was different when Julia was holding his rope and he realized she was there. Now she could be anyplace, maybe far away from him. His earthly senses started to agitate and his breathing quickened. He understood what was going on and gotten himself. As his training kicked in and he assumed responsibility for his breathing, the agitation subsided.

Julia had been only a couple of feet away looking as he managed his dread. She was glad for Robin for how he had trained himself and eventually how SHE had trained him!

The crowd cheered for the first contestant. He was gifted and was progressing nicely. It was hard to beat him and his mistress! Then, the second pair went. They were also excellent, but committed minor errors that Julia was certain would cost them points.

At last, it was their turn!

The first event was an obedience trial. Julia removed Robin's leash from the post and unclipped it from the loop on his cage. Robin was now firmly bound and blindfolded. His task was to follow Julia's commands, precisely. Walk ten steps forward. Stop. Turn right. Stop. Walk in the reverse direction five steps. Robin couldn't see them; however he realized the traps were there, hanging tight for any mistake or misstep. If he committed an error he would fall into a mud trap and need to proceed with the rest of the events canvassed in slime. Julia wasn't allowed to touch him with her hands or her crop. Gradually he went, rapidly because he was being coordinated and if he took too long he would be disqualified. The viewers roared as Robin entered the circle in the center. He had finished the first trial! He stood gladly as Julia came up to him, kissed him, and reattached the leash. Julia stood beside him, maintaining slight tension on the leash. The tension on his rope was significant; it helped him to remember his connection with Julia.

The fourth contestant began, but got confused and went left when he ought to have gone right. He fell into the mud, experienced difficulties getting out and ran out of time.

The last man did great, striding with confidence, and finished the course in record time.

The mirroring challenge was up next. When it was their turn, Julia began strolling gradually while keeping up a delicate pull on the leash. Robin needed to pursue her lead, having just the feeling of the chain to manage him. She turned left, he turned left. She stopped, he stopped too. The judges were searching for more than mere obedience. They were searching for a convergence of the two individuals into a single entity. Robin's task was to understand what Julia needed him to do by the gentlest tug on his leash. He exceeded expectations! It resembled he could read her mind.

For the last challenge, the four remaining men were driven up onto the stage and fastened there. Closed-circuit TV cameras were focused on each of their genitals. Four men, four mistresses. This was the exciting challenge which the viewers of the event would be the judge. The mistresses had two minutes to carry their slaves to maximum excitement inside the chastity cages. The rules were straightforward - No Touching The Genitals! The crowd would pass judgment on which man was bulged the most from inside his steel-walled cock cage. The mistresses knew their men intimately, obviously; however, this was a high-pressure environment and it was hard to tell how each slave would respond.

Julia felt that Robin wasn't focused so she hit his ass cheeks with her crop once. Then again. That is actually what was required, and he now thought of only her. She pressed her body against him as she delicately scratched his lower abdomen with the nails on one hand, and stroked his inner buttocks with the other. She investigated his ear with her tongue as he bulged in his chastity cage. He had a sensation that he was going to break the confinement. The spectators were going wild! The bell rang, denoting the completion of the challenge. The crowd was asked to cast a vote by cheering for each pair in turn. Number one, number two, number three, number four. Robin and Julia got the most intense and loudest praises.

They won!

The head judge moved toward them with their prize: a wonderful high-quality leather collar for Robin's neck. The judge presented it to Julia who gladly secured it onto Robin. She kissed him passionately to rowdy adulation and led him away.

Julia and Robin were buzzing with passionate energy in the wake of winning the competition.

They walked into the room and let the door shut behind them; at last, they were alone. In a flash they were in each other's arms, kissing passionately. All of a sudden, Julia broke the kiss, "Easy now pet, and we have a lot of time for that. I'll come back after I change, why not strip for me". With a grin, she strolled in the washroom.

When she returned, her pet Robin was naked, becoming flushed as she saw him in the flesh and his mind envisioning their erotic adventures. She was wearing a translucent lace top, her succulent bosoms straining the fabric, and a pair of silken knickers, the material sticking to the luscious mounds of her womanhood. The two of them gazed at each other lasciviously for a minute, Robin's cock already throbbing, her lips gradually moistening.

"On the bed, you must assume KARATA for me pet" Julia ordered.

He hopped onto the bedding, and took the position, inclining forward onto his arms, arching his rear end up in the air. His legs widely spread apart; his most intimate parts were left open to her inspection. Goosebumps gushed through his skin, her heart pounded like bass drums imagining their wild and savage forthcoming encounters.

"There's a good pet," Julia stated, laying her had on his head, running it up to his spine, and stopping at the crack of his butts.

"We are going to begin with an assessment. You're offering me your body, and I need to ensure it is worthy of my domination. Today you made your Goddess so proud, but now again you'll have earned your reward. You have such good firm and solid butts," Julia continued as she squeezed his ass cheeks in her grasp, before putting her fingertips between the firm globes.

"What a cute ass you have, pet," Julia teased, tracing a finger around the edge of the crinkled gap, making him groan delicately. His breathing fastened, her hands trembled with excitement. She ran the finger down over his perineum, detecting how sensitive both it and his anal cavity were to her touch.

She took his scrotum in her grasp, crushing delicately,

moving his gonads between her thumb and finger, extending the sac down.

"All appears to be exceptionally sound, my pet," Julia said to Robin, as her hand continued with its descending adventure, fingertips running down the underside of his already hardened cock. She could feel her moisture in between her legs. Goosebumps coursed through her radiant skin.

She grinned wickedly; she was overly pleased as this youthful pet's relentless excitement was absolutely due to her presence, her touch, her exotic voice. Wrapping her hand over his throbbing pole, she expertly started to jerk off him, leaving him completely erect in within moments.

"Mmm... you are a cute sized pet; your Queen is exceptionally satisfied." Julia chuckled.

"Thank you, my queen" the pet answered, reddening at the appreciation, and his exposure.

"Later you'll demonstrate to me how tight your body gets as you cum," Julia teased as she continued to slowly stroke his hard erection, "however you can't cum right now, pet. You should earn your reward by being a sweet young man for your Queen, and satisfying your Queen. So, my pet, do you want to please your Queen?" Julia teased.

"Yes, my Queen," Robin breathed, "I live to serve and satisfy you."

"Great boy, such a lovely pet," Julia praised Robin, gradually masturbating him until she could hear his breathing become heavier and little moans of joy could be heard, before suddenly ceasing her erotic ministrations, leaving his erection hanging agonizingly hard between his spread thighs, the tip gleaming with pre-cum. Rising from the bed and strolling to the dresser, Julia talked back over her shoulder: "Reach behind yourself for me, my dearest, and spread that delightful ass cheeks of yours nice and wide. I want to see your gap open for me."

On the dresser, she opened a cabinet of her favorite lube, liberally covering two fingers with it. Going back to her pet, she saw with a grin that Robin had done as she instructed him to do, his hands pulling his ass cheeks apart. That resulted in the crinkled pink opening between them opened wide for her inspection.

Coming back to the bed, she knelt behind him, appreciating and cherishing him for a second. Smiling to herself devilishly, she leaned down and kissed him between his spread cheeks, her tongue snaking out to press past the rim of his butt.

"Oh, my Queen," Robin screamed in pleasure.

Laughing, she ran her tongue up his perineum over his puckered little star.

"Like that, my slave? If you are good and please me exceptionally, you can have more like these as your treat later." Julia teased.

He tried to reply, yet moaned profoundly as her lubed fingertips discovered his anal cavity in the nick of time. Scouring lube against the outside of his gaping cavity, she thrust one finger inside, gradually sliding it into the knuckle. Pulling back it, she squeezed and thrust two against his puckered hole this time, and grinned down at him. She was immensely satisfied when his hole sucked in effectively both her fingers inside.

"What a good pet, so tight and warm," Julia murmured, "however, I think we'll have to extend you before you're fit to be used appropriately."

She shoved her fingers all through him gradually for a couple of minutes, twisting them as she did, rubbing his prostate, getting intensely stimulated at the vibe of him, and shivering in passionate excitement seeing his nicely extended rim. Then she pulled back her fingers, making him whine marginally in dissatisfaction, his anal cavity closing down tightly feeling the frustrating void.

"Right, where is it, ah this one would be perfect," Julia announced, pulling a medium measured butt plug from her pack. Turning back to Robin she instructed, "Keep those buttocks nicely and widely spread for me darling, I need your anal hole open for this."

Kneeling behind him once again, she shivered slightly as she set the tip of the plug against him. Goosebumps coursed through his skin, Robin licked his parched lips, he gulped hard, his mouth gaping wide as his anal cavity felt the excitement of the alien intrusion in her anal region. Squeezing delicately yet firmly, the tip slid into him, his tight gap stretching around it. She stretched around and stroked his stiffened cock delicately, offering encouragement, while he snorted as she squeezed the plug firmly into his favorite hole. It was heaven; she was taking care of her slave, her pet, Robin.

"Good boy, relax, press back against me, that's my boy!" Julia cooed as the butt-plug's widest point slipped past his sphincter and he squeezed around it hard, with just the flared end left outside.

"Now, we'll leave that there for a while. I need to warm you up some more, externally," Julia chuckled wickedly. "Put your arms underneath your head again and raise your ass up."

As he followed her word by word, she kept on conversing with him.

"You must learn to enjoy your punishment. That's a crucial part of your training, slave. Your rear isn't only for fucking; it will also be for spanking and flogging when I'm disappointed with you. Punishment for my pet in my house is a bare bottom spanking, with either hand, flogger, or cane, equal amounts on every butt cheeks. More serious offenses will result in a double spanking on the base or the standard twenty hits between the legs. Understood?" Julia teased. Robin shivered in passionate excitement.

"Yes, my Queen," the pet swallowed hard.

"Great," Julia answered, grabbing the small leather flogger that she pulled out from her cabinet, "Now, as you've really been a very excellent pet, and this is your training, you will have to take just ten initially. You will count each one before accepting the nest one."

With that, she mightily swung her arm and the flogger painfully landed on his firm ass, making him rock forward in shock. In spite of that, he still obediently counted the agonizing blow.

"One, my Queen," he gasped.

Smack! The flogger smashed into his right ass cheek. It hurt. "Two, my Queen!"

Smack! The burn was starting on his left ass cheek.

"Three, my Queen!"

Smack! Lighting struck again, Julia was impeccably alternating between his ass cheeks. "Four, my Queen!"

Smack! The thunder of the blows was echoing in the room. So embarrassing. "Five, my Queen!"

Smack! The heat was rising. "Six, my Queen!"

Smack! Another flash of pain shivered Robin. Julia was a real sadist. "Seven, my Queen!"

Smack! Like an electric shock, only bigger. Robin was leaking. "Eight, my Queen!"

Smack! Julia took proud in her ass-reddening caliber. "Nine, my Queen!"

Nine later, his ass cheeks were a satisfying shade of red, the crimson hue broken uniquely by the black handle of the butt plug peeking out from between his two-round buttocks...

"I think we're ready now, my pet," Julia pronounced, smiling deviously as she reached out, took the butt plug firmly in her grasp, and all of a sudden, pulled it out of him in one drag. Robin screamed out as his butt all of a sudden stretched wide, and she was delighted to see as she inched closer; that his anal cavity didn't clench entirely, but gaping wide welcoming her presence. He was ready for her.

She opened her cabinet again and took out a blindfold she had purchased particularly for his special and erotic occasion. She moved to sit alongside his head, her lace-covered groin inches away from his face. He groaned softly, he could smell her excitement, he could sense her moistening at his plight. Robin sensed how the delicate fabric followed the mounds of her luscious pussy lips.

As Julia slipped the blindfold on, she whispered in Robin's ear, "The sensations will be electric, my pet. In addition, you haven't yet earned the reward and right of gazing upon my fully naked body for tonight. You'll have to earn them every night. Okay?"

Encased in darkness, Robin had his ears on high alert, hearing just the delicate murmur of ribbon and she slid her knickers off. Goosebumps coursed through his skin and his heart pumped faster because he was so desperate to witness the Holy Grail between her legs, to worship her luscious womanhood! He heard her rummaging in her cabinet, looking for what he sensed would be her strap-on. Robin pondered quietly how huge it would be. He just hoped he would be able to take her, thereby pleasing her. The pet felt the bed move as his Queen moved up behind him; all of a sudden, he was mindful of how naked and vulnerable his private parts were.

Gripping one of his ass cheeks in each of her hands, Julia spread Robin open, moving forward so the very tip of the strap-on leaned against his puckered opening, making him groan in anticipation. Julia shivered in the fire of dominance, Robin shivered in the lust of submission.

"Is this what you want for tonight, my dearest? For your Queen to slide her huge dildo strap-on into your smooth, tight little hole? To use that greedy little gap for my pleasure?" Julia teased.

Robin pleaded, wanting her in absolute desperation, "Indeed, please my Queen, take me, fill my asshole, I beg you to fuck me, my Queen." Robin gulped hard.

"You're such a lovely pet," Julia murmured as she pushed forward firmly yet slowly with her hips, looking eagerly as the tip of the dildo strap-on stretched his young butt hole, the rim growing as she thrust further into him.

Watching with intense pleasure as the smooth rim of his rear-end stretched out as she pulled back the length of the cock, grasping firmly around the pole, Julia started to expertly utilize the full length of her cock to open up his tight youthful rectum. Skillfully utilizing her hips, she shoved somewhere deep inside his butt hole, penetrating her pet with every last inch of the pole.

"Oh! My God, you're so tight," Julia snorted as she drove into him ever more profound, his butt hole gripping the pole tightly, making it press hard against her clit.

In a couple of moments, Julia felt her climax approaching; she had intended to be slow and delicate initially, yet Robin was so tight, and his opening looked so impeccably stretched around her pole, that she really wanted to fuck him hard. For a minute the only sounds were his cries each time she thrust completely into him, the head of her dildo hitting his prostate, and the smack of her paunch and thighs slapping against his body. His throbbing cock and balls swung forward and backward as she fucked him hard, fucked him ruthlessly for her pleasure, pre-cum overflowing from the tip of his erection. As she felt that electric tingle developing between her legs, she forced his butt cheeks as far stretched out as she could, not having any desire to waste even a small inch of the dildo, needing him to feel absolutely full. With a cry, she pushed somewhere deep down into him one final time, cumming hard, gripping his hips and pulling his body back to meet the attacking shaft; impaling his delicate youthful structure.

Breathing vigorously, Julia lay forward, settling upon

Robin's back, strap-on buried as far as possible inside his hot bowels.

"Oh, my dearest, you were so great, absolutely superb," Julia praised Robin as she recovered, and her lips came crashing onto his naked back.

Robin was breathing just as vigorously as his Queen and could just mumble platitudes to her, basking in the warm gleam of having satisfied and delighted her, having unified with her.

After a couple of seconds, Julia kissed his neck, around to his ear, and murmured, "On your back now, my dearest".

Grabbing his hips to keep him still, she gradually began to pull herself back from him, until at last the head of the strap-on showed up from between his anal cavity, his marginally red butt hole glistening with lube between them, open as if pleading for more. He moaned in dissatisfaction, realizing that his thirst would have to be quenched some other time. Robin was disappointed at the feeling that he was no longer unified with his Queen and that she was not inside him making him feel emptier than ever before.

As Robin turned to lie on his back, Julia took the hem of her top in her grasp, and lifted it off over her head, exhibiting her bosoms to him. Finally, he had earned his reward to gaze his naked seduction.

"Wow!" was everything Robin could muster, spellbound by the vision of magnificence before him. Julia was now totally naked, but more gorgeous than ever before glistening in her sweat, infuriating the passion in his eyes, just the thick shaft protruding from between her thighs shrouded her vulva from him.

"My Queen, you look so evergreen," Robin mumbled. She looked between his very own thighs, to his long hard erection, throbbing and leaking, and realized that he meant every word.

Silently she moved back towards him. As she knelt between his legs, he pulled his legs upward, reaching his chest, giving her easy access to his puckered opening. She peered down into his eyes, caressing his cheek with one hand while she placed the tip of the strap-on on against his butt.

"You realize you belong to me, don't you, my pet?" Julia teased Robin.

He could just nod his approval, incapable to turn away from her peering eyes. Gradually, she sank down onto him, the pole of her strap-on sliding effectively into his well-used rear, until her belly squeezed against his, his hard cock squeezed between them, her succulent bosoms against his bare chest. She lay still for a minute, as they kissed passionately, tongues finding one another, and he wrapped his legs firmly around her back.

Gently, affectionately, she started to shake her hips back and forth shoving the strap-on in and out of her pet's lubricated butt hole, making love to him. He screamed with euphoric delight as her cock curved into him, filling his bowel. Pulling her hard against him, he murmured in her ear, "Cum in me my Queen, my Goddess. Cum in my ass-hole. Fill me, mark me as yours. I love you. I love you."

Grinning down at her wonderful and excellent pet, she lifted a bosom to his mouth, moaning with delight as he sucked on her nipple, the snugness of his body already making the dildo press pleasurably against her clit. Her ideal pet would be very much used for her pleasure before the morning and she was certain about that, and she would be intensely and immensely fulfilled. Julia shut her eyes, wondering how she would get him to go down on her with his magnificent tongue for an hour or so later; he would need ample time to recover from the intensity of her thrusts. This would surely be a wedding night to remember for life...a night to live for a lifetime...

Robin never considered the abundance, prosperity, and luxurious lifestyle of his proprietor, Julia. She lived lavishly in a big mansion in Miami and now and then it appears that she had the cash to burn. In any case, Robin never thought of anything that a canine didn't consider. He had been trained as one for such a long time that every single human idea was gone, and everything he could consider was whenever Julia patted his head when she awakened every morning or considered him a good slave after she climaxed all over his face.

Robin loved his owner, and he realized she loved him back too! She was absolutely exquisite. He didn't have any desire to be any other else's property. He was an exceptionally privileged dog.

He generally rested right beside her bed on the floor. She bought him pleasant cozy dog beds that are so delicate and warm! In any case, she generally slept in a big bed which he was hardly permitted to sleep on and that depended on her mood and wishes. Over the last couple of weeks, Robin really hadn't rested on a real. He never considered it in any case since his dog training and pet play began. In fact, he liked his dog beds. He felt as though he was in his place and the place where he belonged.

He always slept so comfortably realizing he'll comply

with her the following day!

"Oh, my puppy! Come to mama!"

Every morning Julia said this in a singing melody voice, ringing a bell she generally had by her bed. Robin sprang up quickly like an excited young pup, desperate for her attention already. Then, when he gazed upward on the bed, he saw one of her succulent udders sneaked out the sheets, while the other was still shrouded under it. He could, in any case, make out her nipples as he crept to her ready to obey anything she would command him.

Robin sat on the floor beside her bed wagging his butt and panting with open mouth and slipped out tongue like a pup as she ran her delicate hands through his hair. She loved to chuckle at his enthusiastic expressions of affection every morning. She looked down to gaze at his hardened erection as she sat with her feet under his cock.

"Awww, I can see a little someone getting excited about a treat," Julia teased. Robin barked accordingly as her toe reached to delicately touch the tip of his throbbing cock. She snickered as a few droplets of cum oozed out onto her foot.

"I think I might have to deal with my pup and his little problem. You've been such a lovely pet!" Julia mocked.

She began stroking his cock with her feet. They were so soft and felt so cozy, it felt incredible and sensual as he desperately humped her feet, already standing on the edge of a mind-blowing blast without it even being a minute yet. Her laughs always sent chills down his spine rippling goosebumps all through his body. He always felt so incredible, cared and valuable to be caressed early in the morning. He realizes she adored him in an extraordinary, yet twisted way. Robin howled and whimpered as he shot cum on the floor and on her soft, sensitive feet.

"Aww, good pup! You like it when mama rubs her feet on that little stiffy, don't you? Julia teased.

Robin enthusiastically wag his ass to express his gratitude as he barked and panted, undoubtedly, that was an incredible, yet an exceptional butt humiliating display of gratitude to his owner. The feeling of her soft, cozy feet always made him yearn for more of her touch. Julia realized her pet's needy glances when Robin stared at her gorgeous, luscious pussy.

"Aww, so my pup loves to see what he sees? He really is desperate to put his little puppy stiffy in here, doesn't he?" Julia giggled.

It was just a minute prior when Robin came hard on her feet, yet her teases were driving him insane and he was soon getting stirred and excited for another round. Julia spread her legs and used her long, sexy fingers to exhibit her perfect pussy. He had already buried his servile tongue in there last night, yet she knew and realized her pet needed and hungered for something more to bury in that Holy Grail of womanhood. Every time he licked her off, he would yearn to pleasure her hole.

"My pup is so demanding animal! I can see you're already hard again for another round! Well, in case you're thinking that I'll use that little stiffy of yours, then I'm sorry to disappoint you. Because, I plan to use your tongue..." Julia chuckled wickedly.

There was no need for Julia to finish that sentence as Robin knew what she really meant and yearned for. He buried his tongue into her luscious pussy, licking and lapping and devouring as if it were his last meal. The smell was like roses, the flavor was so delectable like peaches and creams. He always craved for more of her juices, and she always got certain through his desperate and diligent licks.

"Oh, my puppy...It really seems like you love this more than cumming on your mama's feet..." Julia moaned huskily.

How could she be wrong? She knew Robin loved

climaxing from the strokes of her feet, but sucking, licking and lapping his servile tongue to tribute his Goddess wife was absolutely different. He rejoiced and cherished it more because that was the only possible way to touch her and it seemed adequate for him too.

Julia loved having multiple mind-blowing orgasms every morning. But the only mornings Robin really didn't like were the ones when she would just make him watch her rub and rub consistently for hours, he would drool the while time to devour the palatable juices of her excitement while she loved peeking over at him and seeing the desperate and sad looks all over his face.

"Oh my god…Yes puppy!" Julia moaned and Robin sensed what that really meant. She clamped her thighs down on his face, trapping him there, suffocating him while she rubbed voraciously and violently on his servile tongue as she experienced an ecstatic orgasm. Robin devoured whatever he could, she always came like fountain making it increasingly difficult for him to catch up her breath and coordinate his sucking and licking. He gave her nice slow licks to bring her down gently as she grinned. Robin felt his owner's legs relaxing gently. These were the moments he cherished most as if the world was slowing down.

"Oh puppy…You made mama proud like always…" Julia moaned. "Be in the kitchen for breakfast but not before you clean up the mess of cum you made!"

She extended her gorgeous, sexy legs with her foot inches away from his mouth. It was still dripping with droplets of his excitement. Without a moment's delay and without any further word, Robin licked it all up wanting her ravishing feet cleaned up of his puppy cum. Julia chuckled, gave him the look of passionate adoration, then leaned forward and kissed his brow. Her kisses felt so soft and delicate like pillow.

After Robin licked his cum off the floor, he crawled into the kitchen to discover his owner in a robe. She wasn't wearing any inners. He was amazed and delighted to find his owner preparing the usual breakfast, bacon, eggs, and pancakes. He settled beside her chair on the floor with pleading and yearning eyes.

"Oh, so my pup is hungry? He wants mama's table scraps?" Julia grinned.

Robin spun around whimpering and whining, barking up to her to demonstrate his desperation. Julia's smile broadened. She gave him a half-eaten piece of bacon. Before his lips and tongue wrap around that needy meal, he gave her hand a few affectionate and loving licks to express his gratefulness.

"Aww, you're such a cute pet! Mommy is delighted!" Julia exclaimed.

Once she had eaten her morning meal, Julia rose up on her feet guiding her pet to the couch. She turned on the TV and began to enjoy her morning shows. Robin never saw what was being telecasted, he wasn't allowed to unless he had done something extraordinary to earn his excellent rewards. So, he intently stared at her captivating eyes. When she snapped her fingers in front of her, he crawled to his knees and assumed a position where he can be used as a footrest by her. She laid each foot on one of his shoulders exhibiting her luscious pussy, the most tempting sight that made Robin instantly drool. She undermined his presence while watching the TV. Sometimes, she just loved to forget and undermine her pet's presence, except from the occasional chuckles she gave whenever she would glance at him.

A few hours passed as she sat and watched her favorite morning shows. Julia looked at the clock realizing they were late for something. She quickly stood up and Robin gazed at her ever attentively.

"Pup, go choose some nice dress for me and lay them on my bed. Just the dress, no inners, okay? Then be a good pet and come in here and hold my towel and bath soap," Julia commanded.

Robin shook his head to confirm and enthusiastically wag his ass. He scampered off her room. He chose a lovely, elegant red gown for her with a bow on her back. He carefully took it off the hanger in her closet and laid it out on the bed for her. He then hurriedly crawled to the bathroom and kneeled by the bathtub. He held the towel with his arms and grabbed the soap bar in his mouth.

"Aww, you're such a cute pet! You're so obedient and so special to me! I hope your puppy mind realizes that," Julia teased.

Robin barked jovially through the soap which made Julia giggle. A tear of joy brimmed out of his yearning eyes sensing that his demonstration of enthusiastic affections and strict obedience made him so special in her eyes.

She reached out as he kept the soap in her hand. She scrubbed all over her body making him intoxicated to the lovely smell, but more so in the showers.

"Puppy, shave my pussy. I want it bald and smooth like a baby's bottom," Julia commanded.

Robin was somewhat confused since this task was performed by his owner alone. However, he wasn't in a mood to question her commands and she wasn't in a mood for any bull shits as well. So, he followed her commands. She sat on the toilet spreading her wide as far as possible. He gently scoured a shaving cream on and started to give her pussy a shave ensuring that every little hair was shaved off.

"Goodness, you're doing excellent little pup. I realize you're wondering what all do this might be for, but you will discover soon enough." Julia exclaimed.

Robin wagged his ass as he gazed at her, and he barked likewise as he finished shaving her. He licked away the shaving cream, and from the way in which his tongue lapped her mounds and swayed over easily, she was unquestionably as smooth as possible.

"Good puppy! Truly you are! You're making mommy proud!"

She patted his head as he gave her hand a few enthusiastic licks and wagged his ass. She then left for the bedroom, where she slipped into her elegant dress. He helped her to slip into her heels.

"How does mama look, puppy?" Julia inquired seductively.

She was stunning. Robin hung his tongue out giving her desperate eyes and wagging his butt. His little pup cock jerked and leaked some precum.

"I that that answers my question," Julia grinned. "How about we hop in the car and go for a ride."

They drove for around 30 minutes to an exceptionally extravagant restaurant. Julia glanced at Robin with a wicked smile.

"I will dine in this exotic restaurant. I'll bring you back my leftovers, pup." She asserted.

Before she left, she gave him a soft affectionate kiss on the lips. She had hardly done that in the recent past. Robin froze in excitement. He licked her face as that was the only way he realized how to give kisses and express his excitement.

He sat tight in the car for a considerable length of time. Robin whimpered alone missing his owner as though she was long gone for years. Then when he at long last observed her walking out of the main door, he barked and howled in happiness. But his excitement was short-lived as he froze in sheer terror with a face of profound misery when he saw her holding another man's hand. He whimpered and began crying in deep jealousy and anguish. He was crest-fallen again.

"Goodness, my gosh little puppy! Mommy forgot you were here and I was having exotic supper with Brad. I'm so sorry that I forgot to bring my leftovers!"

Brad and Julia hopped in the car. Robin was making heart-wrenching cries.

"Shhh young doggie, shhh. I'm sorry I forgot about you! But, you should be a good pet and stay calm. Mommy will still arrange for your leftovers."

Robin didn't quite get his owner's words. What leftovers? He might've stopped whimpering, however, he couldn't stop crying. "How could she forget me so easily?" Robin wondered painfully. Julia conversed with Brad on the way back to her stunning house. Just as they pulled up, she turned around and glanced at him.

"Young doggie, be a good pet for mama and head inside while Brad and I talk here for a while. Sit tight for us by my bed. You can win some additional treats and puppy points if you light a few candles and sprinkle flower petals on the bed for us!" Julia commanded.

Every time she said "us", Robin's heart broke as he whimpered and shed more tears. He saw Brad's hand was extremely high up Julia's dress. Robin simply did as he was instructed and crawled into his owner's bedroom. He cherished fulfilling his owner's wishes, so he sprinkled flower petals on the bed, and lit candles. He even played soothing music for them.

He could hear them approaching. The entryway opened and his heart pounded like a thousand drums. When Julia saw Robin, she couldn't help stopping her musings. He must be looking more pathetic than ever before. He was done setting up the room for them to engage in sexual relations and he stood enthusiastically for her, she strolled over to him and got closer to his ear to murmur as she grabbed his cock, which was extremely hard for some unknown reasons.

"Gracious pup. You look so wretched now. Does this make you sad? You're going to watch as Brad fucks mamma senseless, and you will do nothing about it. Be that as it may, I think you secretly yearn for this deep down your heart. Clearly your little young doggie stiffy does." Julia teased.

She stroked his hardened cock a little as he whined; however, he let out a groan. Also, she grinned at me as she stops and turns around to face Brad. She slipped the shoulder straps off as she exhibited her juicy bosoms to him. Brad didn't state anything, but his face said a lot. He massaged and cupped her succulent bosoms in his grasp and then kissed and sucked on them as they fell on the bed.

Minutes felt like weeks, and hours felt like years during their long, hardcore, bed shaking sexual intercourse. Julia groaned noisily, and she came heavily, over and over again. Her face was so radiant through the entire thing that Robin just gazed at her. Undoubtedly, Brad was a champion fucker with a log cock. The manner in which her succulent boobs swayed up and down as she rode him, in the long run, became mesmerizing. They finally came down from the zeniths of their excitements and snuggled in bed with Robin next to her. Julia looked at Robin and her face was lit up like a shining star.

"Oh, yes my young doggie! Your leftovers." Julia asserted.

She patted the bed for her pet to hop on. Robin had never been on it quite recently, and he was unquestionably seeking after it to be on various occasions. The bed was shrouded in sweat and their cum. His owner was drenched. She grinned and spread her legs, exposing her cum filled pussy.

"Go on, little dog, mommy needs to lay down with her man. Lick up your leftovers delicately. Make sure you get every drop." Julia commanded.

Julia's wish was Robin's commands. Her pussy has a musky scent of a potent man's cum that also intoxicated Robin's senses. It also bore the scent of their sweat. She slept soundly with his mouth buried in between her legs. It took him an hour to get every drop and ensure her pussy was perfectly clean. Robin sneaked out between her legs, and he crawled back to his doggie bed. He heard the sheets move as Julia clung to Brad, snuggling him. On his doggie bed, however, there was a note.

"Mommy loves you, little dog."